DEADLINES & RED LINES

STEPHANIE JULIAN

MOONLIT NIGHT PUBLISHING

Finding love one kiss at a time…

Sugar Donahue is determined to live life on her own terms, even if that means working three dead-end jobs to make ends meet. The only bright spot in her day is the moment the hottest player on the Philadelphia Colonials hockey team walks into the diner where she works. Too bad he's so far out of her league he might as well be on another planet.

RJ Mitchell wants Sugar any way he can have her—on a table, up against a wall, whatever he can get. He's at the top of his game and a fan favorite, but his life feels stuck in neutral. He's not willing to risk his heart, but he'll take whatever Sugar's willing to give.

But when eyes meet, and breath stops, and heat sizzles every time they touch, neither can resist the attraction. RJ's been burned by women before and Sugar's insecurities make her feel like she's skating on thin ice. Are they willing to face off at the red line and take the shot, to score the love of a lifetime?

Want to know more? Join Stephanie in her private group, Stephanie Julian Reader Salon on Facebook. And sign up to get all her news at her website, www.stephaniejulian.com

Don't don't miss these other stories in the Fast Ice series:

Bylines & Blue Lines

Hard Lines & Goal Lines

Deadlines & Red Lines

ONE

"Hey, RJ. How's your day going? What can I get you?"

You. I want you. Naked. On the table. Against the wall. I don't care where. And you don't have a clue.

RJ Mitchell made sure his expression didn't reveal the thoughts running through his head as he handed her the menu he didn't need because he knew it forward and backward.

It was Tuesday and The Brig's special of the day was owner Georgie's amazing pot roast. After the workout this morning and the ice time he'd logged this afternoon, pot roast was his reward.

And spending time with Sugar. Can't forget that.

Nope, wouldn't forget that anytime soon. Not when she was always here, serving him at his favorite restaurant in the entire city of Philadelphia.

Pitiful but true.

"Hey, Sugar. It's going. You get signed up for that class you were talking about?"

Her lips twisted and her nose wrinkled in a way that shouldn't have made him think about kissing his way down her naked body. Then again, he'd been lusting after this woman for months, so it wasn't a surprise.

But since his personal life was in limbo or suspended animation or whatever the hell kind of life he was living right now, he hadn't talked himself into seducing her. Yet.

He wanted to. But the situation being what it was...

"Not yet. I know, I know." She held up a hand to stop him from responding, her smile widening. "I'm going to. I just... haven't had the time."

"You need to make the time."

Her smile softened as she nodded. "I will. I just...need to find a couple of minutes. Thanks for asking, though. It reminds me that I need to do it. So what do you want tonight?"

Same answer as before.

He wanted her.

Then ask her out.

He hadn't figured out why he hadn't. Or maybe he knew and just didn't want to admit it.

"I'll take the pot roast."

Her smile widened again. "I knew that. But you never know. One of these days you could surprise me. I'll put the order in and bring back some water. You want anything else right away?"

Yeah. I just don't know if I should ask for it.

"Nah. I'll start with that. Thanks, Shug."

"No problem"

Then she turned and walked away, back to the kitchen. Leaving RJ to watch her walk away. And yeah, he checked out her perfect ass before she disappeared behind the swinging doors into the kitchen.

Yep, he was an asshole.

Jaw flexing, he forced himself to shift his gaze to the front window, where people still crowded the sidewalk on a Tuesday in mid-August. Outside, the temperature still hovered just below ninety degrees at seven-thirty at night, but inside the diner, the air conditioner had to be cranked to subarctic. But it barely made a dent in his internal temperature, which rose every time he was near Sugar.

God damn. If he didn't act on this attraction soon, he was going to lose his mind.

You've already lost that if you think you should be pursuing this woman. She doesn't need to deal with your shit.

Swallowing down a sigh, he flipped over his phone, which had been face down on the table. Most days, he avoided opening social media sites. He had accounts on Facebook, Twitter, and Instagram, but he didn't post a lot. Never had, even before the shit hit the fan last year. Before he'd transferred to the Colonials from LA.

A toxic mix of emotions churned in his gut, pushing past the mental block he'd built for the past fourteen months. Since the night a couple of asshole former teammates took advantage of a couple of drunk women at a party. And fucked the reputation of nearly the entire team. Including RJ's.

The legal battle had been put to rest in California, and RJ had been exonerated. But the court of public opinion had already laid down its verdict: complicit. Not guilty but responsible in some way. Hell, he even thought so himself. Even though he'd tried to—

His hands clenched into fists on top of the table, his knuckles cracking audibly. Taking a deep breath, he opened his eyes and forced himself to loosen his jaw and shove all that shit back down into the pit where he kept it locked up tight.

Giving the room a quick once-over, he decided no one had noticed his momentary freak-out and allowed himself to relax. Just a little. Something he didn't do much of lately. The closest he got to relaxing was having dinner here or hanging with his family.

He didn't have a girlfriend. The bullshit in L.A. had taken

care of that. Marisol had barely hung on two days when the accusations went public. Then she'd bailed. At the time, he hadn't blamed her. Mostly, he blamed himself for dragging her into it with him. Even though he'd done nothing wrong...

He heard the door to the kitchen swing open and his attention automatically shifted.

Not Sugar.

Damn. He definitely needed a hobby other than working out and stalking Sugar.

With a disgusted sigh, he tapped his phone and saw notifications for two texts. Since very few people had his number, it was either family or close friends. Turned out to be both.

`You coming to dinner this weekend? Your sister wants to know.`

RJ huffed out a quiet laugh. His best friend and future brother-in-law, Tim Stanton, knew him well enough to know if Tim invited him to dinner, RJ would be forgiven for blowing him off. But if he blew off his sister, well, that was just a dick move.

The other text was from his mom and, yeah, he'd be a total dick for blowing off his mom.

`Your dad's birthday is next month. We need to talk party plans!`

Shit. Couldn't say no to that either, could he?

Hell, he'd had no plans all summer. Usually, he'd spend most of July beach-hopping with friends and teammates, old and new. Tahiti, Hawaii, Jamaica. Tropical heat, white beaches, drinks with enough alcohol to dull the pain of losing out on making the playoffs, losing the playoffs, or losing the cup. And if you were lucky enough to have won the cup? Well, the alcohol was icing on the cake. Not that he would know. He didn't have a ring. At least, not yet.

"Excuse me, mister. Are you RJ Mitchell?"

The boy stood at least six feet away from his table, probably eight or ten years old. Definitely not old enough to be here by himself.

A year ago, RJ wouldn't have had to force a smile. It would've come naturally. Now, it took a little effort. Even for the kids. And that sucked. It wasn't that he didn't appreciate the fans. After his love of the game, they were the reason he played. Not for fame or money, although he admitted the money was great. The fame, not so much. Especially when you became famous for something you didn't do.

Nodding, he leaned forward a little, not too close, though. "I am. How are you tonight?"

The smile that exploded on the kid's face made RJ's day. Literally, every shitty thought in his head exploded into dust and blew away.

"I'm good. Can I have your autograph?" The kid ran toward his table, piece of paper in his hand. "I have a collection of all my favorite players, but I don't have yours 'cause we couldn't come to the game where the team was signing stuff. My dad had to work, and my mom said we couldn't spend the money on the tickets 'cause then we couldn't pay the electric and—"

"Sorry. Oh my god, I'm so sorry. Danny, I told you to stay in the booth."

A visibly upset young woman with a baby on her hip appeared at Danny's side. Her dark, curly hair and light hazel eyes an exact match to the children, she gripped Danny's shoulder and tugged him back.

"Please, don't apologize." RJ turned his smile on the mom. "Danny told me I'm one of his favorite players. Pretty much made my day."

The woman shook her head, grimacing. "I had to change the baby's diaper and I took the kids into the restroom, but Danny disappeared on me and—God, I'm rambling. I'm really sorry. I told him not to bother you."

"It's no bother. Honestly." Turning his attention back to Danny, he held out his hand for the paper. "You got a pen, big guy?"

The kid's expression fell when he realized he didn't. "No, I—"

"Here you go."

A hand appeared over RJ's shoulder, holding a pen.

Sugar to the rescue.

Danny's smile returned in full force as RJ took the pen and scrawled a short note and his signature on the back of a ragged piece of notebook paper, while the baby squirmed and babbled

and Danny's mom bounced the little girl on her hip.

"Do you play hockey?" RJ asked as he handed back the paper.

Danny glanced up at his mom before shrugging and looking down at his feet. "Nah. Not yet."

And if the mom's expression was anything to go by, not in the near future, either. Hockey was an expensive sport. Skates, sticks, gear, club fees. In a big city like Philly, that could cost several hundred dollars if not thousands. Money some just didn't have.

"Well, you need to talk to your mom about this," he glanced up to make sure she knew he was talking to her and not just Danny, "but I'll be helping out with a clinic next week at University of Pennsylvania. It's free, if you want to try it out."

From the size of Danny's eyes, he really wanted to try it out, and the look he turned on his mom was hopeful.

So RJ directed his next words to her. "A few members of the Colonials are involved, and we provide the kids with everything they need. Equipment included." He didn't tell her they didn't do that for all the kids. He also didn't tell her registration had ended weeks ago. Didn't matter. If Danny's mom said he could go to camp, RJ would make it happen. "If transportation's an issue, we can work something out. Breakfast and lunch included. It's a two-week program for beginners and intermediates."

By the time he finished, Danny's mom actually had a smile and Danny's grin had widened even more.

"If you're interested," RJ pulled his wallet out of his pants and gave Danny's mom a card, the one with his personal email address, "email me by Monday. We'll make it work."

"Thank you. That would be...Danny would love this. Thank you."

"No problem."

"Thank you, Mr. Mitchell. Come on, Mom, let's go tell Daddy."

Danny tugged his mom away from RJ's table, all smiles.

"That was very sweet of you."

RJ looked up to find Sugar standing by his booth, smiling at him. Shaking his head, he picked up her pen and began tapping it against the tabletop.

"Not really."

It'd been self-serving if anything. When you fostered a kid's love of hockey, you grew hockey fans. Major league hockey was nothing without its fans. And sponsoring one more kid was a drop in the bucket for him. Hell, the five kids he'd already sponsored cost less than what he typically spent on suits for the season.

"Yes, it was." She sighed. "Why do you do that?"

"Do what?"

"Put yourself down." One hand went to her hip, which, of course, made him want to look. Which he didn't. "You're such a nice guy."

He shook his head and snorted. "Guess you haven't seen the news in the past year."

She made a little disgusted huff. "Those people don't know you."

"True. But neither do you."

The rhythm of the pen stopped when she put her hand over his. He froze as her fingers curved around his hand, the heat of her skin seeping into his.

He couldn't remember her ever purposely touching him before. Sure, their fingers had brushed when she'd put down plates or taken his glass to be refilled. But she'd never put her hand on his like she was doing now.

Hell, he felt like he was in some period film he'd never watch about Victorians or some religious sect where sex was a mortal sin. He didn't believe in that shit. Sex could be amazing between consenting adults who had the hots for each other.

Of course, the only person he'd had the hots for lately had been this woman.

See? Victorian freaking tragedy.

"I know you well enough. And I think you're sweet."

Looking up, he let himself study her face. When he'd first met her, he'd thought she couldn't be older than eighteen. One of the first times he'd met her, he'd asked what high school she attended. Her nose had wrinkled, and she'd said, *"A tiny one. My graduating class had fifty people. So what're you having tonight?"*

He'd gotten the hint. Nothing personal. Had things changed?

"Thanks. I guess."

Her grin turned wry. "It's a compliment. Take it."

He did. But only because it came from her.

"Thanks."

"Sure."

He smiled back and, for a few brief seconds, they shared a moment. All other sound fell away then: the diner noise, the constant rumble of traffic from the city, the voices from the other guests. They all just faded into the background where they barely registered.

A connection formed, like a string tied around their waists that kept pulling them closer together. It only lasted a few seconds, and maybe he was an idiot to think she noticed anything other than the awkward way he kept staring at her. Like a damn stalker.

Then someone brushed by Sugar, snapping her out of the moment. She blinked, shook her head, and took a step back, like she thought she was too close.

He didn't think she'd ever be close enough. But for her sake, it wasn't going to happen.

"Um, I'm just gonna go check on your dinner."

She turned and hustled for the kitchen like she needed to put out a fire.

Or just get the hell away from you.

Shit.

Sighing, he shook his head as he watched her disappear behind the swinging door.

"YOU SURE YOU'RE OKAY? You look exhausted. With the amount of hours you work, I can't imagine you get enough sleep. You really need to take better care."

Sugar swallowed an exhausted sigh and forced a smile for her coworker. She knew Anika meant well, but the other girl didn't know the meaning of boundaries. And Sugar needed boundaries.

"Long day. Looking forward to crawling into bed tonight."

"I hear you. Big Dude is supposed to have the babies in bed tonight by nine so we can have a quiet night for a change. You know that ain't gonna happen. That man has no spine when it comes to his kids. You just know they're gonna be awake and hopped up on sugar. I don't care if it's summer, they still need to have a set bedtime."

Sugar's smile was natural this time. Anika and her husband, whose given name was John but which no one who knew him ever used because Big Dude fit him too well, had three kids all under the age of seven. They were the sweetest, most adorable kids Sugar had ever met in her life. Their smiles charmed birds out of the trees and candy out of miserable SOBs.

Anika and Big Dude were the kind of parents Sugar aspired to be. Someday. Not anytime soon. She'd raised her sisters until she'd been able to leave home for Philly. She was in no hurry to have kids of her own.

"I agree with you, but Big Dude's not the only one those kids have tied around their fingers."

Anika gave her the side eye as she gathered the plates of her next order. "Are you trying to tell me my babies are spoiled rotten?"

Since Sugar had worked with Anika for the past year, she'd didn't rise to her coworker's bait.

"They're angels and you know it."

Anika grinned her Cheshire cat smile, dark eyes sparkling. "Of course, they are. You need a few of your own."

Sugar mock-shuddered. "No, I really don't. I don't even wanna think about kids right now."

She'd had her fill of changing diapers and wiping runny noses for at least the next ten years. If not more.

"Damn right, you don't need to be thinking about kids," Georgie chimed in from her territory in front of the flat-top. "Let the girl live a little."

Sugar flashed a smile over her shoulder at the restaurant owner, who Sugar owed more than she could ever express or repay. Georgie would probably shut her down fast if she even tried.

"Thank you, boss."

"Uh-huh. Of course, you'd have to get a life first."

Sugar heaved a long-suffering sigh. "Oh, come on, Georgie, not you too."

"See, I'm not the only one who thinks you need to get out more." Anika bumped her shoulder against Sugar's on her way out of the kitchen with her tray. "You need to ask that man out on a date."

Sugar felt her cheeks flame, which she could never hide because her complexion was way too fair. Luckily, she was facing away from Georgie and Anika was on her way out.

"Order up, Shug."

Marquis, one of the other cooks, saved her from the question she knew Georgie would ask. Or maybe saved her from realizing that everyone in the entire diner knew she had a ridiculous crush on a man so far out of her league he might as well be on another planet. Even if he didn't act like a famous athlete who was worth millions.

Gathering the plates onto a platter, she realized it was RJ's order and sighed. Because of course it was.

Pushing through the swinging doors into the dining room, she schooled her face into a pleasant expression and headed back to his table. To the gorgeous guy who made her question every promise she'd made to herself when she'd left her parents' farm in the middle-of-freaking-nowhere northern Pennsylvania.

Rule Number One: No getting distracted by a guy.

Rule Number Two: No getting distracted by a guy.

Rule Number Three: Live your life.

She'd barely made it a few feet from the door when he

looked up. He'd had his head down over his phone, scrolling, but the man had a sixth sense. Probably because of the sport he played. He had to be aware of his surroundings at all times or he could get crushed. When she watched his games, she couldn't believe the amount of punishment a hockey player's body took on a weekly basis.

Of course, the body in question was in peak physical condition—

Shit. Shit. No. Absolutely not. Stop it.

Dropping his gaze, which had caught and held hers as she walked across the diner, she zigzagged through the dining room to the front-corner table, which she now thought of as his. He always sat there, with his back to the wall, facing the front door and the wall of windows. He liked to people-watch. He'd told her so a few times when she'd caught him staring. He'd smiled up at her, that half-cocky grin that made her heart pound and her palms sweat. Not a good thing for a server.

Reaching his table, she smiled at him without meeting his gaze. She'd found she didn't drop as many plates if she didn't look at him. Which was ridiculous. Honestly. He'd been coming here for almost a year. She should be used to him by now.

Like that's ever gonna happen.

Unconsciously, she sighed as she stopped at his table to lay down his plates.

"Hey, Sugar, you okay?"

She didn't have to force a smile this time because he sounded so damn sincere. Like he honestly cared about her answer. Because, damn it, he was just that nice a guy.

Ugh. She needed to get over this crush. It was seriously screwing with her head.

"I'm fine. Thanks for asking. You need anything else?"

And then she made a fatal mistake. She let herself look at RJ. Really look at him. Let their eyes meet, let her smile soften as they stared at each other. And probably let her feelings for him show clear as day on her face.

Their gazes held. She had no idea for how long. Thankfully, she'd already set his plates on the table or they'd probably have ended up on the floor. Because the way he was looking back at her...

Her heart took off, racing like she'd run a marathon.

Was he seriously looking at her like he was thinking the same thing she was? Like he wanted to kiss her until neither of them could breathe and then they would stumble around until they found a wall he could push her up against and—

Blinking, she broke that connection, taking a step away from the table. Which made her feel ridiculous.

"No. I'm good. Thanks."

He drew out that first word for at least three syllables, making it clear to Sugar that he thought there was something wrong with her. And there was.

She had a big, damn crush on the man, and she needed to get the hell over it.

"Okay then." She nodded, still not meeting his gaze. "Just let me know if you do."

Turning on her heel, she forced herself to make the rounds of her other tables before heading back to the kitchen.

And hopefully getting herself under control before she had to face him again.

———

RJ WATCHED Georgie walk to the front entrance, turn the sign from open to closed then lock the door.

She didn't say a word as she walked over to his table and slid into the booth. He still had a hot cup of coffee in front of him, courtesy of Sugar about two minutes ago. He should've left after his previous cup. Hell, he should've left when he'd finished dinner an hour ago. And yet, here he sat.

Less than a year ago, he'd sat in this diner and told his best friend, Tank, he needed to get a life. Today, his sister and Tank were talking about wedding plans for next year. And his younger brother, Brody, and his girlfriend, Tara, had recently moved in together.

Which left RJ at loose ends. Not that he wasn't happy for them. It was just... It left him the odd man out. Again.

Georgie stared at him from across the table, calm and relaxed. He figured she'd perfected that look for years as a sergeant in the Army.

"So. What's eating you? Spit it out."

He appreciated the fact Georgie didn't beat around the bush. If Janine, Georgie's partner in all things, were here, she'd roll her eyes and make sure Georgie didn't overstep. But it was Janine's book club night at the library and Georgie had open ice.

RJ didn't mind. In fact, he appreciated the fact that she looked him in the eyes and confronted him. And that she cared enough to ask.

"Honestly, I'm not entirely sure."

Georgie's eyebrows arched and he saw her lips curl up at the corners. Probably hadn't expected him to answer at all.

"How's practice? I know you've been hitting the ice pretty hard lately. Don't most of you hockey guys take vacation in the summer? Why aren't you on an island somewhere chugging beer and eating all the shit you don't eat all season long?"

That made him laugh, because that was pretty much exactly what most of his team and the rest of the league was doing right now.

"Good question. And one I don't have an answer for."

"That shitshow in LA. seems to be blowing over."

Points to Georgie for describing the situation perfectly. And for not being afraid to mention it. "Probably going to have to go back to testify at some point. But the police have cleared me of doing anything wrong."

"Did you? Do anything wrong?"

She said it so straightforwardly, he almost didn't understand what she was asking at first. His family and his close friends had never once asked if he was guilty of any of the charges laid at his feet. They knew him well enough to know he wasn't. They trusted him.

Georgie had known him a year. And she was the only person who'd asked him flat-out if he'd done anything wrong. Except for the press. They'd hounded him with questions, most of which they phrased to get a specific response. So he'd stopped giving interviews. Until last January when he'd agreed to an interview with *Sports Illustrated* and laid everything on the line.

And things had died down. Mostly.

"No. I didn't."

Georgie nodded, as if she'd already known the answer. "Okay then. So what's on your mind? 'Cause something's definitely on your mind."

Because he knew she sincerely cared, he gave his answer a decent amount of thought. "I feel like I'm stuck in neutral."

Georgie leaned back into the cushion, getting more comfortable. "What are you doing to put yourself back in drive?"

He gave the question some serious thought before answering. "Not a damn thing. I'm just putting one foot in front of the other right now."

"You've been doing that for a year now. Think maybe it's time you veered outta that lane and found a new one?"

"Sounds simple enough. But you know it's not."

"Yes, I do. Have I told you about my first few months after I retired?"

He shook his head.

"I put in my twenty and thought I had the next twenty mapped out. Get a job, settle down, spend my life with the woman I loved. You know, normal shit."

He nodded but stayed quiet, because he was pretty sure she was going to tell him that wasn't what happened.

"Wasted the better part of two years trying to figure out which way I should go because when I got out, I had all these people laying their expectations on me. My brothers expected me to come home and help them with the family business. My grandfather started a Christmas tree farm in the forties and grew it into one of the biggest cut-tree producers this side of the Mississippi. They just expected I'd come home and work with them. Never took into account the fact that that's not what I wanted to do. Then again, I didn't know what I wanted to do. I also knew that if I moved to some bumfuck Pennsylvania town as an Army vet with my girlfriend in tow, I wasn't going to be accepted, at least not right away. And I didn't have the patience for that shit."

"So what'd you do?"

"I moved home. And I fucking hated it."

RJ leaned his elbows on the table. "How'd you get out?"

"Well, first I had to realize I was miserable. And not just because Janine wasn't there. I'd left her in Philadelphia because I knew she'd be unhappy on a farm where the nearest city was a two-and-a-half-hour drive away. But I felt I owed my family, you know? That I needed to be there to help them because they'd held down the fort while I was gone, and it was my turn.

"But one day, my older brother told me I needed to leave. That this wasn't my life and I didn't owe them anything just because this was their life."

"I love playing hockey. That is my life."

"Good. But hockey's not all there is to life."

"Right now, that's all I need."

"What about a week from now? A month? A year? Life's more than just work. I love cooking and I love this diner, but if I didn't have Janine and Wounded Warriors and that damn community garden project Janine started, I wouldn't know what I was missing. And I have a feeling you already know what you're missing."

He didn't know what to say to that because she was right. But he still didn't know what the hell he was supposed to do about it—

"Georgie, you want me to lock up—oh! Sorry. I didn't mean to interrupt."

His gaze snapped to Sugar, who'd just walked out of the kitchen. She'd taken off the apron she always wore and must have brushed her hair and redid her ponytail because she didn't have little wispy curls all around her face.

Then he remembered that Georgie was sitting directly across from him, watching his every move. He wasn't positive, but he was pretty sure Georgie could read minds. And if she'd read his, she knew how he felt about Sugar.

And she'd tell him to take a first step in Sugar's direction. Which was exactly what he wanted to do. And exactly what he shouldn't do. Because Sugar didn't need any more stress in her life and his life was constant stress.

"No problem," Georgie answered. "And yeah, I think I'm gonna hop outta here early. Janine's been bugging me to go to some exhibition in Olde Town, so I think I'll surprise her at the library and we'll head down to that."

Then Georgie turned her attention back to RJ and he knew exactly what was about to come out of her mouth. His brain began to spin excuses faster than his body reacted to a cross pass from a winger.

"RJ, you mind staying a few extra minutes, just until Sugar's done? Don't want her to be here all alone. Juan's already left for the night, kids are sick, and I gotta skip out now if I'm going to make it to—"

"Sure." He looked straight at Sugar. "No problem."

Sugar's eyes widened then she blinked and dropped her gaze to the floor. "That's okay. Really. I'll be fine. I don't want to make you—"

"I've got nowhere to be. It's not a bother."

"Great." Georgie slapped the table. "That's settled. Thanks, Sugar. You're really helping me out here. And RJ, I appreciate you not leaving Sugar alone. I'm sure there won't be an issue, but it'll make me feel better."

Knowing he'd get to spend time alone with Sugar made RJ feel instantly better. Screw the fact that just minutes ago he'd been worried Georgie would figure out he had a thing for Sugar. Right now, didn't matter one bit.

"Happy to help," he said. "I don't have anywhere to be tonight."

Which was the god's honest truth. And if he was being completely honest with himself, he'd much rather spend a few minutes alone with Sugar than head back to his apartment. Alone.

Hell, he couldn't even adopt a dog because he wasn't home enough to take care of one. Just one more thing he'd had to sacrifice for his career. Because he didn't have anyone else in his life. Spending a little alone time with Sugar might actually make today less pathetic.

"I'm gonna get out of here." Georgie slid out of the booth. "Thanks again, kids."

Sugar seemed frozen for several seconds, looking like she wanted to say something. But she must have thought better of it because she simply turned and headed for the kitchen without a word. A few seconds later, Georgie yelled "Good night" from the pass-through window behind the bar, then he heard a door open and close somewhere in the back.

A few minutes passed, but Sugar never reappeared. He heard her moving around in the kitchen, dishes clattering, glasses ringing, silverware clanging.

Are you just going to sit here?

No. He wasn't.

TWO

Sliding out of the booth, RJ walked to the swinging doors that separated the kitchen from the dining room and stepped through into the kitchen. Where he found Sugar wiping down a gleaming stainless-steel table countertop with a rag.

"Need any help?"

She jumped a bit, but he didn't think he'd scared her. Hell, he hoped she wasn't afraid of him.

Throwing him a quick smile over her shoulder, she shook her head.

"I'm good, thanks. I'll just be a couple minutes. You really don't have to wait. Georgie's just overprotective."

"She cares about you. That's not a bad thing."

"I know. And I'm grateful. But I really am capable of taking care of myself."

"It's not an imposition. I'd just be home watching TV anyway."

Her hand slowed on the counter and, finally, she turned to face him. Their gazes connected and held, heat rising from his gut to spread through his body. But mainly gathering in his cock.

He didn't dare adjust himself and draw her attention to his growing hard-on.

"Well…thank you. I don't mean to sound like I don't appreciate it."

"Not a problem."

And it wasn't. Not at all.

Even if there was no way in hell he should slake his burning lust for this woman.

Finally, she nodded, her gaze falling away. "Okay. I'll just be a few more minutes. You want something to drink while you wait?" She paused and flashed him a quick smile that made the heat in his lower body burn even hotter. "I could make you a quick milkshake."

His grin caught him off guard.

"Although…that's probably not allowed in your diet, is it?"

Was she teasing him? She looked totally serious, eyes wide. But the hint of a smile at the corners of her lips gave her away. He felt his own grin widen.

Go ahead. Admit it. The only reason you come here so often is because of her.

"The occasional milkshake isn't going to kill me. Sure. I'd love one."

Her eyes widened a tiny bit more, like she hadn't expected him to agree. Then her smile exploded, and he felt like he'd been punched in the gut. Literally. Like someone had taken the butt end of a stick and shoved it into his stomach.

"Okay. Mint chocolate chip, right?"

Fuck. She knew his favorite ice cream flavor.

And it probably didn't mean a damn thing. She was a waitress at his favorite restaurant, where he ate more than he ate at home. But…he could count on one hand how many times he'd ordered a milkshake here. And she'd remembered.

"Yeah. Mint chocolate chip. Sure."

"Okay. One milkshake coming up."

She turned and headed for the other side of the room, to a walk-in freezer.

He probably should've headed back to the dining room, sat at the counter, and waited for her to bring the shake out to him. But a tiny part of him rebelled against leaving. That stubborn, stupid piece of him that'd kept him in L.A. longer than he should've stayed. When he'd refused to see the writing on the wall. He should've known his time with the Regents was over the second his teammates had stopped looking him in the eyes.

He'd thought he could ride it out, that it'd blow over. Because, damn it, he hadn't done anything wrong. But the men who'd known him and been his friends for years had turned their backs on him and treated him like a criminal. Not all of them. A few had stuck by him. But most had avoided him like he had the plague.

Starting over in Philly had been the best thing he'd done.

Wanting to kiss Sugar right now was the worst thing he could do to her. Because she didn't need to get caught up in his problem. Just the fact that she was younger would start all the rumors swirling again.

Of course, being alone with her was the complete opposite of staying away.

Shit.

She returned from the freezer with a carton of ice cream and headed for the counter and the blender. His hands tightened into fists because he absolutely wanted to put them around her waist and pull her against him, feel her slim curves plastered against his body.

She'd been his obsession for months. One he'd tried to hide. One he shouldn't allow himself to indulge.

Not doing such a good job of that, are you?

Hopefully Sugar wouldn't pick up on it.

Maybe you want her to.

No. No, he didn't.

Fuck. Yes, he did.

His jaw locked as his gaze followed her every move. What the hell was it about her that made every part of his body burn? It made him ashamed of his complete and utter lack of self-control. He was a grown man, for Christ's sake. He should be able to control himself.

He should just turn away.

That's what got you into this whole mess in the first place.

He realized he was grinding his back teeth and had to make a conscious effort to unclench his jaw. He'd gotten better at letting go of the anger that'd been eating away at him since he left LA. But it wasn't gone completely. It lingered in the back of his brain like a—

"RJ, are you okay?"

Sugar stood a few feet away, milkshake glass in her hand, concern in her big green eyes. Concern and...something else. Something that looked an awful lot like desire.

He took the glass out of her hands, operating on autopilot.

"Yeah. Thanks."

She swallowed, hard. And blinked. But didn't look away. Then her lips parted, like she was going to say something. And closed before she did.

The urge to kiss her flared into a red-hot ball of lust that lodged in his gut, an aching mass that clawed at him to do something. Lean forward, press his mouth against hers and kiss her until he couldn't breathe. He wanted to suck all the goodness out of her, because she'd taste as sweet as her name. He just knew she would. He'd kiss her until he drained her dry.

And it still wouldn't be enough for him. Because he was an emotional black hole at the moment, and she didn't deserve the shitstorm he'd bring her way.

Clamping down on the urges pushing him to bend down and take what he wanted, he deliberately straightened, putting several inches between them. It emphasized the differences in their height and made him painfully aware of their differences.

At six-two and two-twenty, he knew how to use his height and weight to his advantage on the ice. Off the ice, those things didn't usually come into play. But around Sugar, he was painfully aware of both. She reminded him of some fairy freaking princess, all long legs and arms, slight frame, blonde hair and pale green eyes. If she came into work wearing a flower crown and a Ren Faire costume, he wouldn't blink an eye because it wouldn't look out of place on her.

He should chug the damn milkshake and get brain freeze. Maybe that would help.

Maybe you should just dump it down the front of your pants.

When he lifted the glass to his lips, she blinked then looked away. Fast. And turned to go back to wiping down the counters. They spent the next few minutes in silence, and he tried not to be an ass about it, but he couldn't not watch her. Finally, he just gave up trying.

She moved like she'd done this a hundred times before. Efficient and fast, even though she had to be tired. She'd been on her feet for the past eight hours at least and, except for the way she occasionally kneaded her neck with her hand, she didn't look tired.

Then again, she never looked less than perfect to him. She could be coming off a twelve-hour shift in the dead of summer and he'd still want to drag her up against his body and kiss her until neither of them could breathe.

So do it.

Why did that not sound like a bad idea now? It should be. It should be a horrible idea.

"RJ? You ready to go?"

His gaze locked with hers, and he was pretty sure the world kind of stuttered to a halt. It was such a weird feeling, he actually shook his head to see if he was having some kind of weird balance issue.

"Yeah. You're finished?"

She shrugged. "I have a few more things to do, but you really don't have to wait any longer. You know I live in an apartment right next door, right? I'm just going to run this last load through the washer then I just have to set the alarm, lock the door, and walk about five feet. You really didn't need to stay. But...I appreciate you taking the time."

He wondered if she appreciated anything else about him. Or if she just thought he was a creepy older guy watching her every move.

"Don't have anywhere else to be. Besides, if Georgie found out I skipped out early, she'd never let me live it down."

Another one of her bright smiles lit up his world, chiseling another chink out of the wall he'd been rebuilding around his desire for her.

Honestly, just give it the hell up already. The world isn't going to come crashing down if you kiss her.

He really wanted to kiss her. And right now, she didn't look like she'd object.

Pushing away from the counter where he'd been leaning, he closed the distance between them in a few steps. Her eyes widened, but she didn't move away.

"Can I ask you a question?"

She didn't answer immediately, her lips pressed tightly together. He really thought she might actually tell him no. Instead, she nodded after a several long seconds, her head moving slowly, as if she were still weighing her decision.

"If I kiss you, are you going to smack me?"

Her eyes widened even farther. "Why would I do that?"

"Because you don't want me to kiss you."

"Who says I don't want you to?"

"Do you?"

She swallowed hard. "Do I what?"

"Want me to kiss you?"

"Do you want to kiss me?"

"Yeah, I do. I have."

"So why haven't you asked before now?"

His lips curved in a hard grin. "Maybe because I wasn't sure how you'd respond."

Her brows rose and her expression made it clear she thought he was lying. Or, at the very least, trying to pull one over on her.

"Are you trying to tell me you were worried I'd say *no*?"

"Of course."

She didn't say anything for several seconds and he waited for her to say whatever was on her mind. Because she definitely had something she wanted to say.

Her smile vanished, but he had no idea what she was thinking.

"And if I say no?"

"Then I walk out the door."

Another pause that made his gut tighten into a knot.

"I'm not going to say no," she said. "Because if I did, you'd walk out the door. And I don't want you to go."

"Are you saying you want me to kiss you?"

Now she smiled, one of those wide, bright, sunny smiles, the kind that drew him in like a tractor beam. The kind he'd been obsessing over since the day he'd met her. Well, almost since the day he'd met her.

The first time he'd stepped into this diner, he'd been so damn preoccupied with his own problems that he'd barely registered her presence. It wasn't until the second time he'd stepped through the door that he'd noticed her. He hadn't stopped since.

"I don't want you to go. And yes, I want you to kiss me."

SUGAR FELT like she was vibrating from the tips of her toes to the top of her head.

RJ Mitchell wanted to kiss her.

Kiss. Her.

If she didn't pass out before he actually got around to it, she may even enjoy it. Not that she thought he'd be bad at it. She didn't think RJ was bad at anything. And if he was as good at kissing as he was at playing hockey... Well, hell. She might just spontaneously combust seconds after his lips touched hers.

Because, holy wow, she'd been thinking about kissing him for months. Since the first minute he'd walked through the door of the diner and slid into the booth across from Tank, who'd been the first famous person she'd ever met.

RJ had been the second. And if he kissed her, he'd be her second at that, too. Which was kind of pathetic for a twenty-three-year-old. But she'd never thought, never dared to hope that RJ Mitchell would *want* to kiss her. Even after getting to know him over this past year, she'd never expected that.

Hell's bells, she hoped she hadn't scared him off because he continued to sit there and stare at her. She was about to say something, anything, to get him to move—and he did.

He wrapped one big hand around the back of her neck, fingers weaving through her hair. He didn't pull her closer and he didn't shift into her space. He just continued to stare into her eyes with that same intense, laser focus. That gaze made heat bubble low in her body, kinda like lava in a volcano. Red-hot and slow-moving but powerful enough to make her quake. Every muscle felt taut and stretched to the limit. Her stomach tightened into a ball and her heart beat in a rhythm she didn't recognize.

She wasn't afraid. At least, not of him. Maybe she was a little afraid of how well she'd match up to other women he'd kissed, because a guy like this... He had to have kissed a lot of girls. Like...a lot. A guy like this, rich and famous, never lacked for companionship.

And now he wanted to kiss her. There was no way in hell she was going to say no.

She just didn't want to be bad at it. Especially not with RJ. Who had a look in his eye she could honestly admit she'd never seen on another man in her life. She wasn't completely inexperienced. But even though she and her former boyfriend hadn't been angels, they'd also been teenagers. And teenagers were notoriously horny. You definitely couldn't call them knowledgeable. Enthusiastic, yes.

But when Bobby had died—

RJ lowered his head and covered her mouth, and everything in her head shut off like she'd flipped a switch.

Because RJ was kissing her.

In the dark in her apartment, in bed and alone, she'd dreamed about this. Dreamed about how his lips would feel against hers. The man had the most beautiful mouth she'd ever seen, which, yeah, was weird but still...

And he kissed her just like she'd imagined he would.

Perfectly.

Her eyes snapped shut, which made it even better. Because it just did. With her eyes closed, her senses were heightened. She breathed in and his scent infused her brain, making every muscle in her body loosen like she'd taken a k-pin. She felt like she could melt into him, like butter over hot corn on the cob.

Wrapping her arms around his neck so he couldn't get away,

she leaned in closer, wanting more. Still hardly believing this was happening because, oh my god, RJ Mitchell was *kissing* her.

And he seemed really into it, too. Like he'd been wanting to kiss her until it felt like an ache in his gut and he had to kiss her or he'd just wither away and explode into dust. Right now, though, she felt like she could burn to a cinder. His lips moved against hers with purpose, the heat of his body a spark set to inflame her lust. She wanted to grind her hips against his, to see just how much he wanted her. But he kept one hand on her hip, holding her just far enough away that she couldn't grind against him.

And maybe that was for the best. Because even though they'd known each other for the past year, they didn't really know one another.

Well, they were getting to know each other now. And she'd learned the man knew how to kiss. He used his mouth as well as he used his hockey stick. With a skill that took her breath away. But she sensed frustration in his kiss. Or maybe it wasn't frustration but something else. Something darker. Something that made her want to put her hands on him and pet him.

So she did. Spreading her hands across his back, she smoothed them down as far as she could reach. But she got distracted when RJ used his hand to angle her head to let him kiss her deeper. He didn't have to ask twice for her to open to him. When he licked at the seam of her mouth, she let him in.

And shivered as his tongue slid into her mouth and teased hers. Although teased wasn't the right word. No, he was deadly serious. It was like they'd skipped over the teasy, flirty part of courtship and moved straight to the hot-for-you, need-you-now portion of the date.

Of course, this wasn't a date. This was a stolen kiss in the kitchen of the diner where she worked. She still wore her uniform of black shorts and white tank top, both of them skintight because, yeah, she liked the way she looked in them and it brought her more tips.

And because she wanted to look good for RJ. Who kissed her like he wanted to strip her naked, set her on the prep table, and screw her right here and now. Which she would have no problem with. None. Even though she'd have to spend another hour cleaning the damn kitchen—

He released her mouth and she might have whimpered in protest. Her eyes flew open and her gaze connected with his and held.

"You still with me, Sugar? Because—"

She practically yanked his head back down to kissing distance and just before their lips melded, she swore she saw him smile. That smile... It meant everything. It wasn't smirky. It was almost relieved. It made him even hotter than she already considered him to be, and, trust her, she figured RJ could make sparks with a wet paper bag.

But now those sparks made her reckless, ready to push forward and damn the consequences. Tightening her arms around his neck, she went onto her toes as his hands spread across her back then skated down to her hips. She was ready and willing when he lifted her off her feet. Without thinking about it twice, she wrapped her legs around his hips as his hands slid to her ass to hold her against him.

He moaned deep in his chest, his hands clenching as he pulled her closer until she thought she could feel the heat of his erection between her spread legs. She was probably just imagining that but, damn, she wanted to feel his cock pressed against her. The man filled out a pair of jeans like nobody's business, and yeah, she'd looked, front and back.

One of the first things she learned about hockey players... They had massive thighs. Muscular. Thick. And big hands. And biceps that bulged, threatening to tear the seams on his t-shirt sleeves. Or, at the very least, stretch them out of shape.

RJ had the strength to hold her and not act like he was exerting any strain at all. She wanted to climb the man like a tree and beg him to screw her on the nearest flat surface and she didn't care how long it would take her to clean it.

You wouldn't have to clean anything if you invite him up to your apartment.

RJ tilted his head, deepening the kiss again. Her body shook; she felt like she was being consumed by heat. She couldn't imagine what she'd feel like if they ever actually got naked.

When. Not *if* they got naked. *When.* This was going to happen. She wasn't about to let this man get away from her now when she had him almost exactly where she wanted him. Because the way he made her feel, the way his lips moved over hers and how hard his fingers dug into her thighs, it was obvious he wanted the same.

Now, maybe the blood rushing to critical parts of her body, like her clit and her nipples, might have something to do with her surety that she'd have this man in her bed, splayed out on top of her and making her beg him to come.

Hell, she might come if he moved his hand just a few inches forward so the tips of his fingers could brush against the seam of her jeans, currently pressing against her clit and making her wet.

Her hips shifted, pressing her mound against his stomach and making her shudder with a lust so strong, she moaned. RJ's hands clenched, pulling her even closer until her breasts were plastered against his chest.

Now, the heat increased. Her skin tingled and so did every other part of her body. It'd been a year, at least, since she'd been this close to a guy. And that'd been a disaster. This...wasn't. No, this felt great. Amazing. Better than amazing. It felt fucking awesome.

Opening her mouth to the advance of his tongue, she felt him sweep into her mouth, licking, tasting. Her arms tightened around his neck as her head tilted to give him more access, encouraging him to continue.

He shifted her weight in his arms, wrapping one strong arm around her waist, freeing up one hand, which he put to good use. First, he stroked his hand up her back, making her sex clench and her body shake. The sound that emerged from her chest might have embarrassed her if she'd had the brain power to think about it. But RJ had pretty much blown her mind by this point.

She shimmied closer, her hips shifting as her clit throbbed. And when he wrapped his hand around her ponytail and tugged, not hard, just enough to let her know he was in charge, she wanted to surrender.

His kiss became slower now, as if he'd realized she wasn't going anywhere and he wanted to torment her. She was okay with that as long as he didn't stop. As if he'd read her mind, he pulled away, breaking the seal of their lips. Her eyes flew open and got caught in the sky blue of his. The intensity of his stare made her stomach clench in reaction.

"Why did you stop?"

It was the only thing she could think to ask because she totally wanted him to continue.

"I need to see your face when I ask you my next question."

"Okay."

Please let him ask to come up to my apartment.

"Are you sure this is what you want?"

She was so hot for him, she couldn't think of anything to say other than, "Absolutely."

His smile was slow, but it had a wicked edge that made her core clench and her breath hitch.

"Glad to hear it."

"Do you really have to ask? Just the way I look at you should've given me away. I thought you weren't interested so I tried not to embarrass you with my stupid crush—"

"I'm not embarrassed. Not at all."

She grinned and watched his gaze drop to her lips. Swallowing hard against an almost overwhelming rush of desire, she tightened her arms around his shoulders and sank her hands into the short strands of his hair. He'd recently had it cut, which of course she'd noticed. He'd let it go during the end of the season until it'd brushed his collar. But now, it was cut short on the sides and back and a little longer on the top so his bangs brushed his brows.

He was the most handsome man she'd ever met, and she still had a hard time believing he wanted to kiss her. He was an honest-to-god star athlete and he'd had his tongue stuck down her throat not five seconds ago.

"Come home with me."

Her lips parted in shock at his rough, growly request. She'd almost convinced herself he was going to set her on her feet, tell her he'd made a mistake and walk out the door. That he'd realize she was so *not* on his level and chew off his arm to get the hell away from her.

"My apartment's closer."

His grin felt like a caress against her skin. "If you're sure you're okay with that."

Another flash of heat from that grin made her want to fan her face. "I'm definitely okay with that."

"Then lead the way."

It took her a second to loosen her legs from around his waist so he could set her feet on the floor. It took an embarrassing couple of seconds for her to get her feet moving.

But when she did, she couldn't get out of that kitchen fast enough.

RJ KNEW Sugar lived above the diner in one of the apartments, but he hadn't wanted to invite himself up. He didn't want to be that guy.

But you're the guy who's going to follow her up the stairs to her bed, aren't you?

Yeah, he was. Because he wasn't going to miss the chance to have Sugar.

And Sugar certainly wasn't acting like he was coercing her. No, she'd taken his hand and was tugging him toward the dining room and the front door.

The dining room was dark, the only light coming through the front window. It was close to eleven-thirty at night, but it was summer in the city, and people still cruised up and down the sidewalks. With a few practiced moves, she opened the front door, waved him through then followed him out and locked the door behind them.

She didn't say anything, but she grabbed his hand and tugged him to the left, toward the wooden door that separated the diner windows from the windows of the vintage record shop next door. Opening that door with a key, she pushed through, smiling up at him with a grin that made his dick harden even more than it already was.

He followed, because there was no way in hell he wasn't going to follow her anywhere she went. Inside, the narrow hall was brightly lit, almost too bright. But of course, Georgie and

Janine wouldn't allow any dark shadows in their building. Especially not when they knew Sugar lived here alone.

Sugar led him past the two apartment doors on the first floor to the stairs then up to the second floor, where there were another two doors. She headed for the one directly off the stairs and unlocked that. Pushing it open, still holding his hand, she stopped and turned back to look at him. Head cocked to the side, eyebrows raised, her expression held a dare. Almost as if she didn't think he was going to follow her inside.

He wasn't stupid. He stepped over the threshold, pushed the door shut behind him, and reached for her again. Gripping her around the waist, he lifted her into his body, her arms wrapping around his neck again. She anticipated his next move, her head tilting to the side so he could kiss her again.

Christ, he could kiss her all night and not get tired. She gave him all of her, didn't hold anything back. And he gave her everything. He poured every ounce of desire and frustration and need into his kiss and she took it in. Which made him burn.

Opening his eyes for a split second, he spotted the nearest wall and took two steps forward so he could put her back against it. Pinning her to the wall allowed him to free up his hands. Because he had plans.

He spread his hands on her hips then slid them up her body, stopping just before he reached her breasts. Her body surged under his hands, pressing into his touch. The sound she made in her throat made his cock respond with a jerk. Her head tilted to the side and she kissed him harder, dragging him even farther under her spell. Her body heat seeped into his, and his hands tightened on her body. Her breasts beckoned, and he filled his hands with them. Standing next to him, her head barely reached his chin, but what she lacked in height she made up for in curves.

Hips, breasts, ass. The girl was stacked. And totally not his type. In California—

No, he wasn't going to think about that part of his life. Not now. Not when he had this woman in his arms and her tits in his hands and her mound pressed against his stomach as she kissed him stupid.

And yeah, she'd taken over the kiss. Her fingers had slid from his shoulders into his hair and she gripped the strands, tugging his head to the side so she could get a better angle on his mouth. He grinned into her kiss, let her control it for several long seconds while he rubbed his thumbs over her nipples poking through the thin cotton of her shirt and bra.

She was so fucking soft, he wanted to strip her down and run his hands all over her body.

When she sighed into his mouth, he squeezed. She rewarded him with a low moan and tightened her hands in his hair. She wriggled even closer, her legs tightening around his waist. And shutting down every last hint of resistance he might've had lingering on the edges of his consciousness.

He'd leave if she asked, but he was pretty damn sure they'd passed that point downstairs. Hell, his mind had been made up from their second meeting.

Lifting his head, he looked down at her, made sure she was looking back at him before he spoke.

"I'm going to put you down but only so I can take your clothes off. You okay with that?"

Her smile was a thing of beauty.

"Okay. As long as I get to return the favor. Put me down."

He took his time, smiling for the split second it took her to unwrap her legs from around his waist. He didn't release her immediately. He held her against him for several seconds before he let her slide down his body. The zipper on her shorts brushed against the ridge of his cock, making all the muscles in his body taut, almost to the point of pain. Hell, his erection was going to have the imprint of his zipper on it by the time he let her put her hands on it.

Right now, he'd deal with it because it kept him in check, at least somewhat.

By the time her feet hit the floor, his smile had disappeared, and she had her teeth lodged in her bottom lip and her fingers dug into the muscles of his shoulders. Her eyes rounded, and her smile disappeared as soon as she stood. He couldn't decipher her expression. Then her hands stroked down, over his pecs, and her gaze followed.

He realized he'd been nowhere near as hot as he could get. Because the feel of her palms flattened over his nipples held a sense of pleasure he'd never encountered before. Not with any of the women he'd been with before. And despite the fact that he could've had a different woman in his bed every week in California, he'd never been into meaningless sex.

He had to have a connection with a woman he had sex with her. Some of his friends had ragged him about being a priest, but emotion played a big role in sex for him. Which was probably why it'd been a while since he'd taken a woman to bed. He hadn't had the stomach for it.

Watching Sugar watch her hands as they followed his body down to his waist made emotion churn in his gut. Lust, need, anticipation. A healthy dose of *holy shit, finally.*

Reaching up, he framed her face in his hands, rubbing his thumbs along her cheekbones. Her skin felt like silk, but he knew there'd be even softer places on her body. And he wanted to explore each and every one of them.

Her hands reached his waist and slipped under the hem of his shirt, her palms flattening on his sides then sliding around to his back. Lightning flashed beneath his skin, a visceral reaction that made his lungs seize.

Glancing up at him, she looked at him from beneath long lashes. The heat in her gaze seared him straight through to his gut.

"You're so hot."

Her voice held a hint of amusement, but he'd blown past the banter stage minutes ago. He didn't think he had it in him to be playful. Not anymore. He wanted her hands stripping away his clothes so he could do the same to her. Right fucking now.

"Then we need to fix that."

Reaching behind his head with one hand, he gripped the back of his shirt and drew it over his head. He dropped it on the floor to the sound of Sugar drawing in a deep breath. Okay, that made him smile, because he knew she liked seeing his naked chest. Her eyes widened and she stared for a few seconds before looking up again. The smile on her face had faded, but her hands gripped him tighter, nails digging into his skin, sure to leave little half-moon bites.

His grin returned, this time with a harder edge because lust was kicking him in the ass. It was all he could do not to strip her right here and take her against the wall. Which could be fun but definitely not long enough.

He wanted to take his time. Wanted to be sure he savored every single moment.

Cupping her face in his hands again, he began to lower his mouth to hers.

They both froze as her phone rang.

THREE

Sugar seriously considered ignoring her beeping phone because, now that she'd gotten her hands on the man who'd starred in every one of her dreams for the past year, she didn't want to take her hands off and risk him getting away.

Then again, she couldn't simply ignore it. What if it was old Mrs. Miller, who lived in the next building? What if she'd fallen again? What if it was Sun or Carlos who lived in the apartment below hers? What if it was Georgie or Janine?

What if it was her parents?

At least that would be easy. She'd call them back tomorrow.

"Do you need to get that?"

RJ's voice rubbed against her senses, raising goosebumps and causing her thighs to clench. From the first moment she'd seen him walk into the diner, this man had gotten under her skin and stayed there.

Looking up into his eyes, she shivered at the desire burning there. For her. He wanted *her*. She'd almost wanted to pinch herself but that would look pretty stupid. And she didn't want to look stupid in front of RJ.

"No." *Ugh.* She pulled the phone out of her back pocket, taking a step away. "Well, let me just check it. I can't believe—"

Oh yes, she could believe. She sighed at the name on the screen. Her sister Cookie had always had the damn worst timing in the world.

Swiping the call into voicemail, she set her phone on the nearest flat surface and looked up at RJ. Who continued to watch her with a look that made her want to grab his hand and pull him back toward her bedroom.

Oh damn.

"You're not going to fit in my bed."

The man's smile lit her entire body on fire. It just wasn't fair that anyone had that kind of power, but apparently, he did. And she was going to enjoy being burned to a crisp.

"I like a challenge."

She reached for him, the low tone of his voice and the look in his eyes a lure she couldn't deny. He let her lace their fingers together, let her walk into him until she could feel his hard-on press against her stomach. He didn't try to hide it, and for some weird reason, she was reminded of the difference in their age.

She knew, from checking his stats on the Colonials website, he was thirty, halfway to thirty-one. At twenty-three, she knew women her age who might think he was too old.

She definitely wasn't one of them. Older guys usually had their shit together. And for all the crap he'd been through in the past couple of years, RJ had kept his shit together. She admired that about him.

Hell, she thought it was amazing how he'd managed to stay a decent human when stupid people were saying so much crap about him.

"I'm not much of a challenge," she said. "I'm pretty much a sure thing."

That made his smile widen into a grin that took her breath

away. Putting his hands on her forearms, he guided them around his waist then put his arms around her shoulders. He leaned down to kiss her and just before he did, he said, "Keep saying things like that and we won't make it to the bed."

He fit his lips over hers again, and this time she realized he'd been holding back on her before. Maybe he hadn't wanted to frighten her. Maybe he just hadn't been sure of how she'd respond.

Now, she knew exactly what he wanted and she had to push aside the momentary insecurity that cropped up. She hadn't dated in a while. Okay, technically, it'd been almost two years. Since she'd moved to Philly, she'd been too damn tired to even think of dating. The one time she'd even considered it a couple months ago had been a disaster.

And then she'd met RJ and the thought of dating anyone but him had just seemed like too much work. Now here he was, kissing her, their tongues entwined and his hands pressing her closer, his cock an insistent pressure against her belly.

She gripped his waist, his bare flesh burning her palms. Then she felt his hands tug the hem of her tank top out of her shorts. She had way too many clothes on, and the couch was much closer than her bed.

Since he had his back against the wall, she pulled away, tugging him with her as she headed for the couch. Her apartment was tiny, but that meant she didn't have a lot of furniture to worry about. The couch that had come with the apartment was a sectional, and it had wide, soft cushions.

He obviously realized where she was leading him, and in the next second, her feet left the floor again. Her startled laughter rang through the apartment, but it was quickly cut off by a moan when he fastened his teeth into her ear and bit down.

Her breath caught in her throat as he stopped at the couch and let her slide down to her feet. His hands smoothed around her waist to her stomach, pressing her back against him. This position felt so much more erotic because she couldn't see him.

Except...she could.

She'd left the blinds up, and there was just enough of a glow from the kitchen light that she always left on that she could see their reflection in the window. She couldn't see their faces, just their bodies. But that was more than enough to make her sex clench.

She stood in front of him, but the man was so big, she could see his outline around her. She saw his hands on her body and the tilt of his head, angled down toward hers but not touching.

Oh god, she was going to suffocate if she didn't get air into her lungs. One of his hands flattened against her belly to hold her back against him. They stood that way for several seconds, and she realized he must be watching them, too.

"I think we'll just stand here for a few minutes."

His breath brushed against her ear as he spoke, and she had to swallow before she could speak.

"I'm good with that."

"Glad to hear it."

She shuddered, her sex clenching, as his hand began to move, making a circle on her belly before moving slowly upward. It didn't take long for her body to decide it liked this. A lot. His fingers reached the underside of her left breast and brushed the sensitive curve. She sucked in a breath, her stomach contracting as his other hand skimmed down her hip to brush the bare skin of her right thigh below the hem of her shorts.

The warmth of his skin felt like a brand, but he didn't linger. His hand lifted back to the waistband of her shorts where he flicked the button out of the hole and slid the zipper down in one smooth movement.

The snick of the zipper releasing sounded loud, sending all her other senses into a tizzy. Her lungs stuttered, and when she drew in a breath, all she could smell was him, which made her physically ache to feel his hands on her bare skin.

But RJ seemed determined to go slow. Her experience with guys wasn't huge, but she couldn't believe how carefully he was treating her.

"You know I'm not going to break, right? You need to go faster."

His huff of laughter raised the hair on her neck and sensitized every inch of her skin.

"Oh, I know you're not going to break. But I'm definitely not rushing this. Where's the fun in that?"

"I think we'd have more fun naked."

Another laugh. "Still plenty of fun to have before we get to being naked."

She could barely breathe but still had to respond. "I think I need to be convinced."

Without warning, he opened his mouth on her neck and fastened his teeth into the curve of her neck and shoulder, and, oh holy hell, her thighs clenched like she was a freaking virgin. Her lips parted on a gasp as he began to kiss his way across her shoulder, while his right hand began to work her shorts over her hips.

They were so tight, they dragged her underwear along with them. Or maybe that was his goal all along. Whatever, she was naked from the waist down when she opened her eyes again. His right hand was spread across her belly, his pinky nearly brushing the short hair on her mound. As she watched, his left hand cupped her breast and squeezed, stealing what was left of the air in her lungs.

She only started to suck in air when his hand at her breast began to knead, almost distracting her from the slow glide of his hand down her stomach. His fingers tugged at the hair on her mound before continuing its journey down.

Her clit ached with anticipation, but he carefully avoided it and instead used his hand to spread her legs farther apart. She did what he wanted, leaving her pussy exposed and so sensitive, she swore the air brushing against it could make her come.

She knew it wouldn't be that easy, but when RJ cupped her, letting his fingers slide along her slick folds, her pussy contracted, practically begging to be filled.

"RJ."

"You're so wet. And so warm."

"Then do something about it."

She moaned in frustration when he moved his hand back to her stomach. "Damn it—"

And her knees nearly gave out when he tweaked her clit followed by the press of his fingers at the entrance to her pussy. The hand on her breast moved so he could squeeze her nipple between his thumb and forefinger just as he slid a finger inside her sex.

Her head fell back against his shoulder and she would've curled into herself, but he wouldn't let her. He released her breast so he could wrap his arm around her chest and held her tight against him while he slid a second finger between her legs and into her body.

His fingers were thick and rough and felt amazing as he pumped them inside her. Her pussy gave way as he forged ahead and clenched around him when he tried to retreat.

"Jesus, Sugar, you feel amazing."

"So do you. Don't stop."

"I won't. Not until you come."

At the rate he was going, that wouldn't take long. She couldn't believe how fast he'd gotten her to this state. Not that she had a lot of experience, but before, it'd taken her a little while to get primed.

Realizing she'd closed her eyes, she opened them so she

could see what he was doing to her and found him watching. Without thought, her right hand reached up to hold on to his arm encircling her shoulders. Her left hand rested against his left forearm, feeling the muscles flex as he fucked her with his fingers.

The sensation of being penetrated by him was enough to make her doubt that she was actually awake. She'd dreamed about this, but the reality was so, *so* much better. The heat of his body burned against her own skin while being held so tightly against him, unable to move, thrilled her to her core.

And being able to watch him was a turn-on she'd never understood until just this minute. Erotic to the point of being almost embarrassing. But it wasn't. God no. It was amazing.

"Do you like what you see?"

She blushed, though she knew he couldn't see it in the dark. "Yes."

"Good. Because I want to watch you come."

As he spoke, his fingers stroked high inside her and at just the right spot.

And she gave him what he wanted.

RJ FELT Sugar's pussy clench around his fingers a split second before her eyes closed and her head fell back against his chest. Her moan reverberated through his chest and straight to his cock.

His entire body ached with lust, and his cock fucking *hurt*, he wanted her that badly. But he didn't turn her and lift her onto his rock-hard erection. No, he watched her come around his fingers because, holy fuck, she was fucking beautiful.

At some point, her hair had come loose from her ponytail and now framed her face, messy waves erotic as hell. For some reason, so was the fact that she still wore her top. He'd take care of that in a second, but he was still enjoying the feel of her arousal and the clench of her pussy around his fingers.

He stroked her a few more times, drawing out her orgasm. And when she finally began to melt back into his body, he slipped his fingers free, tugged her shirt over her head and released her bra with a flick of his fingers. Her breasts practically fell into his palms.

"Damn, you're pretty, Sugar."

Her eyes fluttered open and she stared into his in the window. "You need to be naked. Now."

He grinned, though it looked more like he bared his teeth because he wanted her so much. "You're right. Give me a hand, will you?"

He meant those words however she wanted to take them. Apparently, they amused her because her lips curved in a seductive smile as she shook her head so her hair fell back over her shoulders.

"Absolutely."

But first, she toed off her shoes. When she turned to face him, she was completely naked, and she'd lost the smile. But the look in her eyes was pure heat.

He thought about looking in the window to check out her ass, but he couldn't look away from her eyes. She had him pinned in place. And when she reached for the button on his jeans, he froze, not wanting to give her any reason to stop.

She didn't fumble but she didn't exactly go fast. That was good and bad. Bad because it took longer, but good because it was torture. Really good torture.

His cock was so hard, she had to release him slowly because the stiff rod pressed tight against the zipper. When she had it lowered all the way, he wanted her to slide her hands inside and grip him tight. Instead, she flattened her hands on his abs and leaned forward to press her lips to his chest.

Forcing his feet to stick to the floor and his hands in fists at his sides, he felt fire spread from every point of contact. From her hands, unmoving, to her lips, which were moving. She kissed her way across his chest to his left nipple, licking at it before taking the tip between her teeth and nipping at it. It was his turn to suck in air through clenched teeth as every muscle in his body tensed in expectation of her next move.

She took her own sweet time stringing a line of biting kisses back across his chest to his other nipple. By the time she arrived, he thought he might come on her stomach.

He managed not to embarrass himself that badly. But it was a close call. By the time, she lifted her head from his chest, he'd reached the end of his rope. Taking a step back, he bent to untie his sneakers then toed them off and tossed his jeans on top of them.

When he straightened, he caught Sugar taking a good look at him. He didn't know if she started at his feet, but she definitely didn't lift her gaze to his immediately. She took her own sweet time checking him out. By the time she finally met his gaze, he was grinning and so was she.

He liked that she wasn't shy or coy about sex. Marisol had made sex a special event, like she had to perform in a certain way to make him happy. A few other women had acted like they were auditioning for a soft-core porn movie, all breathy moans and dirty talk.

Sugar felt real. Natural. And he couldn't want her more.

"The bed's back that way."

She nodded to her right, her breasts bobbing as her hands settled on hips.

"Condoms?"

"Drawer in the kitchen."

His smile widened. "Why are they in the kitchen?"

Her shrug looked a little sheepish. "Because I've never opened them and that's just where I stuck them."

"We need to crack that seal."

Before she could answer, he scooped her up into his arms and lifted her against his chest, startling a bark of laughter from her as he turned and walked toward the tiny kitchen to the left of the front door.

"Which drawer?"

She pointed and he stopped in front of the only three drawers he could see. Twisting in his arms, she reached for the top one and pulled it open. He didn't see what she was doing because his gaze was locked onto her breasts. He'd never considered himself a breast man before. Sugar was changing his mind.

Hell, Sugar could probably change his mind about a lot of things.

And that probably wasn't something he wanted to broadcast.

"RJ."

His gaze lifted back to hers and caught her grin before she tried to hide it.

"Mission accomplished."

He really liked this girl.

"Not yet."

Her grin disappeared altogether, but that wasn't a bad thing. Because all of a sudden, the atmosphere shifted from fun to deadly serious. They were naked and he had a raging hard-on and she had a box of condoms in her hand. An unopened box.

"Open the box."

She blinked, like he'd surprised her. It took a second, but she finally tore off the plastic, opened the box...and pulled out at least ten condoms.

"I guess we can start with these."

His laughter caught him off guard, though it shouldn't have. He'd laughed more with this woman in the past hour than he had the past year.

"I hope I can live up to your expectations."

She looked like she had something she wanted to say but was biting her tongue against it.

"What?" he prompted.

"I don't need you to live up to my expectations. You already exceeded them."

The absolute truth in her tone stunned him for half a second. Then his lust came roaring back and he slammed his mouth back on hers and kissed her until he literally couldn't breathe. Her bare skin against his body lit him on fire and he broke off the kiss so he could see to walk to the couch.

He set her on her feet before he dropped onto the couch, leaned forward, and lifted her over his lap. Sugar didn't say anything, her only response a quick intake of breath before her hands landed on his shoulders and her legs parted so her knees hit on either side of his thighs.

"I think we'll only need one for now."

She nodded, tore one off the strip, and threw the others over her shoulder. It would've been amusing if everything weren't so urgent right now.

His cock fairly vibrated, he was so hot for her. and when she tore open the packet, his balls tightened in warning. He had to consciously loosen his fingers at her waist, because he didn't want to leave marks on her skin.

His gaze locked on hers as she withdrew the condom. Even when she dropped her gaze so she could roll it down his cock, he watched her face. Her fair skin was flushed with heat and her teeth were lodged in her lower lip. Concentration made her brows draw together as her fingers smoothed the latex over his rock-hard cock.

Her tentative movements didn't register right away. He was enjoying the hell out of having her hand on the most sensitive part of his anatomy. But when she released him, he looked up to find her watching him.

"Don't stop."

She blinked. "What do you want me to do?"

He thought about his answer for a second because now she looked a little uncertain. And he didn't want there to be any uncertainty tonight.

"Whatever you want."

Her head cocked to the side, as if she didn't quite believe him.

"I want you."

His heart twisted in his chest. "I'm right here and I'm not going anywhere. Come closer."

She leaned forward, tentative now, her hands settling on his shoulders. He didn't know what had happened, but he wasn't going to let her lose her confidence now.

Cupping her face in his hands, he rubbed his thumbs over her lips, their softness a tease he couldn't resist. Drawing her even closer, he put his mouth over hers and devoured her.

He slid his tongue between her lips and enticed her tongue to duel with his. She responded immediately, her fingers digging into his shoulders as her head tilted to the side so he could have easier access. The longer they kissed, the more he felt her soften. Scooting closer, he felt the heat of her pussy as she hovered over his cock. It would be so easy to just position his cock and settle her onto it and thrust until he got off. But he didn't want to rush her. He wanted her with him for every step.

So he let his hands smooth from her cheeks down her neck to her shoulders then down her back. Her body shifted beneath his hands, like a cat looking to be petted. She arched toward him, her breasts pressing against his upper chest.

His right hand shot back up, cupping a breast and squeezing before pinching the nipple between his thumb and forefinger. Her moan rocked him to his core, making lust race through his body like a flash flood.

The hand on her hip tightened as he drew her closer, easing her down until the slick lips of her pussy settled against his erection. His cock pulsed at the contact, and he groaned into her mouth, his hand tightening on her breast before he forced his hand to relax.

He didn't want to hurt her. He was bigger and stronger, and she felt so small against him. But there was a part of him that urged him to continue, to take everything she was offering. He'd give her back what he could, though he wasn't sure it'd be enough. He wasn't sure he had it in him to give her anything but an orgasm at this point in his life.

Which made him a dick.

No, it made him like every other guy he knew who wanted sex without a relationship.

Shoving aside those thoughts for now, he put his concentration back where it should be...on Sugar. Or more importantly, on making Sugar come.

She'd started to rock against him, rubbing her sex against his cock, making his hips rise to meet hers. In a split second, control of the situation seemed to shift, giving her the power. Her hands slid into his hair and gripped the short strands, tugging to pull his head back and twisting her head so she could deepen the kiss.

For several seconds, he let her take it. Let her rub against him, pull his hair, and press her breasts against his chest. Until he just couldn't take it anymore.

With a few quick movements, he released her breast, grabbed his cock, and tilted her hips until he had the tip of his cock positioned at the entrance to her body. He heard her soft gasp and felt her body still, although her lips were still pressed against his. Everything narrowed down to the sensation of his cock head poised to breach her.

Lifting her head, she opened her eyes and looked into his.

"Do it."

He hadn't been waiting for her to say something. He figured they wouldn't be here if she didn't want him here. But hearing her say those words gave him a thrill like no other.

She was giving him permission and he was going to take it farther than she'd ever been.

Pulling her down, he watched her face as his cock stretched her open, sinking deeper as he let gravity do some of the work. She blinked as he held himself rigidly still then began to tilt and rock down his cock. It took every ounce of his control not to move and bury himself as deep as he could too fast. He wanted to be fucking her but he also just wanted to feel her wrapped around him, to soak in the sensation of her heat and the tight muscles of her pussy clenching around him.

It wasn't long but it felt like hours until she finally took him all in, to feel the short hair of her mound tease the base of his cock. To hear her breathing become faster and harder and see her eyelids lower until he could barely see her eyes.

Her hands laced behind his neck and she released a soft little sigh when she finally had him completely encased. Then she leaned down and rested her forehead against his.

"You need to move or I'm going to crawl out of my skin."

"I like where I am at the moment. You're so damn tight. You feel amazing."

"So do you. But I need you to move."

"Go ahead. Take what you want."

She hesitated but only for a second. He had a split second to wonder if she was going to go shy on him again...and then she moved. She rolled her hips, just a slight motion that anyone watching might have missed.

It blew RJ's mind.

"Ah fuck."

He clamped down on his first instinct to take over, watched as her eyes glazed over then shut as she continued to make those slow, almost hesitant moves. It was torture. It was heaven.

Every sense heightened. He heard every breathy gasp, saw her teeth lodge in her bottom lip and worry it until he leaned forward and sucked it between his own lips before several seconds before letting it go again.

Her hips rolled forward sharply, drawing a groan from him and sinking his fingers deeper into her skin. His cock pulsed, and now his hips lifted slightly, making her suck in a breath and rise with him.

It didn't take them long to find a rhythm because she'd already started one. He just joined in like they'd been practicing this for years. He thrust and she sank. He withdrew and she rose. Every motion caused his cock to harden more than it already was, more than he'd ever been before.

His eyes tried to drift closed, but he wouldn't let them. He wanted to watch her response, wanted to see how his every move affected her. When he thrust up, her lips parted to draw in air, and when he pulled away, she frowned, just a tiny little motion of her brows drawing together.

He became fascinated by her response and moved hard, faster. Got a thrill from watching her that he'd never had before. Every little thing she did made him want more.

She made him feel alive again. He chased that feeling.

He followed her lead, let her set the pace. Slow and steady at first, she wound him up but provided no release. His desire spiked, hot and hard. His cock stiff as an iron pike, he soaked in her heat, let it seep into his blood and spread from his head to his toes.

Her cheeks flushed and her hair messy around her face, he'd never seen a more erotic sight in his life.

"You're so beautiful."

Her eyes widened and she swallowed hard as she sank again and paused. Her breasts rose and fell with every agitated breath, drawing his gaze. Leaning forward, he pressed his mouth against each mound, then kissed his way up her neck to her mouth, where he let himself drown in her sweetness.

When he drew back, her eyes stayed closed for several seconds before they opened slowly. Her expression held a carnal heat that hadn't been there before, which totally flipped his switch.

With one hand on her chin, he pulled her close and kissed her as his other arm wrapped around her waist to hold her tight. This kiss held a command that she immediately answered. He felt her surrender in the way her body melted into his, in the way she arched closer and took him just a tiny bit deeper.

And then he took control.

With his arm at her waist, he lifted her up then pushed her back down. Her pussy clenched around him, tight as a fist, demanding he give her more. Give her everything.

The hand on her chin slid around to her nape so he could hold her steady while he kissed her. While he fucked her.

Sugar made a sound low in her chest that reverberated through his body. He hadn't thought he could get any more excited than he already was. He was wrong. He let instinct take over, let it guide his movements. But he couldn't get enough leverage in this position.

In a split second, he rose to his feet, still lodged deep in Sugar, and took them to the floor, Sugar still on top. He wrapped one arm around her waist and the other around her shoulders, keeping her body tight against his.

Deeper. Yes. That's what he'd needed. In this position, he could get so deep inside her.

He held her so tight, she wasn't able to move. At first she squirmed, trying to match his pace, but finally, she gave in and let him control her completely.

Every upward thrust, he heard her suck in a breath and realized he'd found the perfect angle. The base of his cock teased her clit every time. Her body began to tremble and finally, her pussy clenched around him as she began to come. The rhythm of her orgasm finally managed to push him over the edge, and he groaned as he came, the arm around her waist holding their hips together tight.

FOUR

Several long moments later, after they'd finally caught their breath, RJ lifted Sugar off his body, groaning a little as his cock slipped from her tight sheath.

She made a little sound of disapproval but went without a fight. Sitting up, he gathered her into his arms and rose up until he could set her back on the couch. Then he stood, slipping off the condom and asking where the bathroom was.

Forcing her eyes to open, she waved a hand toward the tiny bathroom across from her bedroom.

Sugar thought about moving, thought about walking to her bed but couldn't muster the energy to move. She'd never had sex like that in her life. And she'd certainly never had an orgasm that powerful just from penetration. Her former boyfriend had had to play with her clit for minutes to get her come. Luckily, they'd been young and enthusiastic, though inexperienced.

RJ was *not* inexperienced. A little alarm bell rang somewhere deep in her brain, but she ignored it. Nothing was going to come between them right now. Not one damn thing.

RJ was gone for only a minute or so, and when he returned, she let herself look at his naked body without a shred of embarrassment. Considering what they'd just shared, she felt she had the right to look.

Damn, the man was built like a god. Tall and lean but muscled. And those thighs. She remembered now how he'd used just his legs to rise off the couch and get them to the floor and her mouth watered. By the time her gaze reached his face, he wore a grin and her cheeks flamed. And not because she was shy.

"You okay?"

His voice, deep and warm, hit her in the gut like a fireball and spread outward, rubbing against every nerve ending and making her want to jump his bones. Again.

Smiling, she nodded, hoping she didn't look like an idiot. Instinctively, her hands went to her hair, no longer contained by the braid. She worked her fingers through the knots, which could only get worse if she left them go. Her hair was so thick, she sometimes thought about getting it cut off. But then she'd think about her tips...

"I'm fine. My hair's just—"

"Perfect."

He reached the couch and sat next to her, perfectly comfortable in his nudity. And no reason for him not to be. The man was better than fine. He almost must've figured if she was looking, he could, too, because now his gaze slid down her body before meeting her own eyes again.

"Beautiful."

He made her feel that way, even though she knew she was a little on the skinny side. Yeah, her boobs were decent, but she knew sometimes she could look like a stick figure.

"Come here."

Then again, if he didn't mind...

He was reaching for her before she'd even started to move, his hands lifting her onto his lap. The heat of his thighs burned under hers as she wrapped one arm around his waist and let the other rest against his chest, where her hand petted the fine mat of hair on his chest.

"I've wanted to do that," RJ said, "since the first time I saw you."

Her head popped up so she could see his eyes, because that sounded like one hell of a line. But the sincerity in his voice and his expression made her toes curl.

"Let me take you out to dinner tomorrow night."

Her brain stuttered for several seconds, wanting to say yes immediately. But she knew she couldn't.

"I'd love to, but I can't. I've got work."

"Thursday?"

She shook her head. "Working."

"Are there any nights you *don't* work?"

SUGAR'S HAND stopped making little circles on his chest, and RJ wanted to kick his own ass.

Shit. That'd sounded like an accusation and he certainly hadn't meant it to be one. He just wanted to see her again. As soon as possible.

Now he sounded like an entitled prick.

"I work 'til ten tomorrow, and I work a split double Thursday. Friday and Saturday nights, I won't be done 'til two in the morning."

"The Brig isn't open that late. Where else do you work?"

He wasn't sure if he imagined it or if she paused before answering. "I pick up shifts over at Breyer's on South Street. And I waitress in the lounge over at Nero's Club on the weekends."

Shit. The words on the tip of RJ's tongue were some of the stupidest he could say so he bit them back before they could escape. Because he had no right to say them.

He had no right to question her choice of employment. Not everyone had it as good as he did. Some things came easily to him. Like his profession. He was a damn good player. Some of it was probably genetics, but mostly, he worked his ass off to be the best damn offensive player on the team. He drove himself to be good. And along with that skill came money. Even if he never played another game, he'd never have to worry about how he was going to eat.

But he wasn't clueless. He knew most people weren't as well off as he was. He knew Sugar was one of those people. It didn't mean a damn thing to him. He liked to think he was a decent guy. He had good friends and he genuinely liked most people. And none of his former girlfriends and lovers had ever accused him of being a possessive asshole.

But he hadn't known Sugar worked at Nero's. He'd been there. He knew what went on in the private lounges on the second floor. He'd been to a few private parties there, but he'd always left before the true partying had started. The drugs and the sex.

RJ didn't consider himself a prude, but if not wanting to drink until he passed out or have public sex with women paid to be there gave him a reputation for being a stuffed shirt, he could live with that. Which was why the accusations in California had been such a kick in the gut. Because he wasn't that person.

He didn't want Sugar to work at Nero's.

All of that flashed through his brain in about ten seconds while she lay with her head on his chest and lightly dragged her nails though the hair on his chest. When she lifted her head to look up at him, he was gritting his teeth so hard, he thought he might actually crack a few.

Her brows lifted. "If you've got something to say, go ahead and just spit it out. Don't let it fester."

He considered his options, but really there was only one thing he could say. "I've been to Nero's."

Her brows rose like he'd said something stupid. And maybe he had.

"I work there. I know what goes on upstairs. I only work the first floor, never the private parties, although the other girls say you can make good money if you do. I'm not interested in being some rich dude's toy for the night. The money I make waitressing in the main bar a couple nights a week pays my rent for the month. A couple good nights and I can pay my utilities, too."

Choose your next words carefully.

It was something he'd heard his mom say during his teen years, mainly to his brother and sister, but also to him a few times. It reminded them to take a breath and think. Good advice for this moment.

"Do you *want* to work there?"

Probably not the best choice of words, if the expression on her face was anything to go by.

With a little sigh, she shimmied off his lap, and it took every ounce of his self-control not to wrap his arms around her and keep her there. But that would be a total dick move. So was the fact that his cock was already rebounding. Not a shock, really. He hadn't had sex in months and he'd been lusting after this woman for a year. Of course he wanted her again.

But the look on her face made it clear she wasn't thinking about sex right now. Grabbing her underwear off the ground, she pulled it on, then grabbed his t-shirt and pulled that over her head. Claiming it for her own. He liked that.

"Not everyone has their career path figured out by high school," she said as she sat on the opposite end of the couch, not far enough that he couldn't touch her but definitely not in his lap. Where he wanted her. "Or the ability to jump into their dream job at eighteen."

He nodded. "I know. I know how lucky I've been. But...do you want to be a waitress for the rest of your life? Or is it just a job?"

"Are you trying to ask me what I want to do with my life?"

"I guess so...yeah."

Sitting cross-legged, she put her hands on her knees and stared into his eyes. "When I was a kid, the only thing I wanted to do was live in a big city. I grew up on a farm in the middle of freaking nowhere. My mom's family owns one of the largest food supply chains in the northeast. My dad inherited a fortune in oil shares. They met in graduate school. Mom's got a master's in psychology. Dad has a master's in environmental economics. They got married and decided to buy a farm and be hippies. Luckily for them, they had the money. We always had food and clothes, but my parents kinda went overboard on the whole 'make your own path' thing."

"How so?"

"Oh, just that they let us do whatever the hell we wanted and as long as we weren't in danger of hurting ourselves, they didn't care. The problem was, I did."

"You're the oldest?"

She nodded. "Yeah. Of five. My parents realized I was more of an adult than they were when I was, like, eight. My youngest sister was one, and one day my mom handed her to me. And then my mom went back to working in her garden and my dad retreated to the barn, where he smoked a lot of weed and tinkered with the plow that he used to take us for rides in the fields."

"And you took care of your younger sisters."

She shrugged. "Of course.

"Firstborns."

Her smile burned. "That's right. You are too."

He nodded. "Yep. There's definitely something to be said about birth order affecting your personality. Gabby, my sister, was easy, but Brody," he shook his head, grinning a little, "he could be a holy terror. During the season, when my dad was still playing, sometimes we wouldn't see him for a couple weeks at a time. For us, it was normal, because we didn't know any different. My mom was always home with us and, and with three, overachieving kids, it was more than a full-time job for her to take care of us. I tried not to be a pain in the ass."

"Did you always know you wanted to play hockey?"

"Yeah. I mean, when you grow up with a dad who plays professionally, of course, you think about it. And when you realize you've got some skill... It's kind of a no-brainer."

"Did your parents ask if you wanted to play, or did they just assume?"

"My dad was always really careful not to influence either way, but Brody and I both knew it's what we wanted to do."

"And it worked out for you, so there's that."

The teasing note in her voice made him smile. Hell, he'd smiled more with Sugar than he had in the past eighteen months.

"Yeah, it has. Probably has a lot to do with genetics and then just being around the sport as much as we were, you're bound to pick it up. Even if you choose to do something else, you're still gonna learn how to skate and hold a stick, because that's what your dad does. You know?"

She shrugged. "Not really, no. I mean, my parents hired people to work the farm, so my mom spent a lot of time in her garden. I used to spend time with her there, until I realized she mostly wanted me to keep my sisters occupied. She loves her plants. She has huge gardens, and she's always growing all sorts of weird things she gets from all over the world. But I think she loves those gardens more than she loves her kids. Especially when they got older. My mom loves babies. Until they can talk. Then she kinda lost interest."

Sounded like Sugar's mom wasn't Mother of the Year material. And it was definitely not his place to say anything to criticize her mom. Time to change the subject.

"So how are classes going?"

Smooth move, asshole. Nice transition. Probably gave her whiplash.

Her lips quirked up at the corners, and her nose did an adorable little wrinkle thing. She knew what he was doing and she was considering if she wanted to let him get away with it. Fair enough.

"Slowly," she said finally. "With my work schedule I have to be careful I don't take too many classes. Most of them are online, but I don't want to fall behind and not be able to finish."

Smart. But he'd realized over the past year that Sugar wasn't just a pretty face. When he'd happened to catch sight of her on break, she was usually reading something on her tablet, usually for homework.

"I get it. I take a few classes every summer, just core requirements. I figure when I'm not playing anymore, I'll have time to take a full course load and get my degree."

Her brows rose in surprise. "What are you majoring in?"

"Sports management."

"Ah. I guess that's kind of a no-brainer, huh? Wait," she held up one hand, "I don't mean you don't need a brain to study it. You know that, right?"

His grin widened. "I know what you meant. And yeah, I guess it is. I mean, I'm not sure what I want to do when I can't play anymore, but I know I want to be involved with the sport in some way. So I figure I should learn how to do that before something happens and then I'm not prepared. I went straight into play after the draft. I knew college wasn't going to happen right away."

"Was that how you planned it? Did you want to go to college?"

"I thought about it. Talked to my parents and they said they'd support whatever decision I made. I think the first serious draft discussion started when I was fifteen. I'd just been drafted into the OHL and it never stopped. By the time my draft year rolled around, I knew I was getting drafted. I didn't know how high, but I knew I was going to play right after high school. I didn't bother applying to college."

"Did your parents want you to go to college?"

"If I had decided I wanted to go to college, they would've made that happen. I could've been drafted and played college hockey for four years. But they know the game. If you're good enough to get drafted in the top ten, you're going to play next season, whether it's with the AHL or the NHL. My dad got his degree the same way, taking classes over the summer. I knew I could do it."

"How high did you get drafted?"

"I was second."

"Wow. That's amazing. I mean, I'm not surprised, but that's really huge. Isn't it?"

"It was. The press were all saying I'd go first or second, but I tried not to get too caught up in the hype. There were a lot of good players that year and the first pick that year was a goalie."

"But you're one of the best players in the league right now. Right?"

Coming from her, the compliment was appreciated. From anyone else, it might've made him brush it aside. "I'm good at my job."

The look she gave him was wry. "You're more than good."

She said it so matter-of-factly, he smiled. "Thanks. I work hard and I love to play."

Not a lie but not exactly the truth, either. He'd lost his love of the game for a while. Perceptive Sugar picked up on what he hadn't said immediately.

"That mess in LA affected your relationship with the game, didn't it? I mean, it's understandable, considering what you went through last year."

There was no curiosity or hesitation in her voice that indicated she doubted his innocence. She'd never once looked at him like she thought he'd done anything wrong. She believed him. There were few people who had that level of trust. Then again, it took a lot of trust to bring someone into your bed. At least it did for RJ. He suspected it was the same for Sugar.

It made him realize just how much this woman had come to mean to him over the past year. He'd have a shitty day, and he'd walk into the diner and see her and immediately everything would be better. Or at least it would for as long as he was there with her.

For months, he'd fought against the thought that another person could cure his problems. He never wanted to drag anyone else down into his shit, not after what had happened with Marisol.

"I honestly can't believe anyone thought you would hurt someone like that," she continued. "I mean, that's just crazy talk."

He grinned and watched her gaze drop to his lips before lifting back to his. "Why is that crazy talk?"

"Because you're a freaking boy scout."

"I never had time to be a boy scout."

She gave him a look he knew well from his sister, one that said if he wasn't careful, she'd smack him. He'd rather she punished him in other ways. Since he was naked, she'd be able to see exactly what he was thinking if he wasn't careful.

"You know what I mean," she said, shaking her head. "You're almost too good to be true."

"No, I'm really not. I've got faults."

She shook her head slowly, as if to make sure he understood what she was saying. "I didn't say you were perfect. No one's perfect. You're just..."

When she didn't continue, he said, "What?"

Her smile broadened, the hint of sass enough to make his heart pound faster and his cock thicken. He couldn't be this close to the woman who was wearing his shirt and a pair of panties and nothing else and not want to get inside her again. Maybe this time they'd make it to the bed. The thought made his cock hard as stone.

"You're just yummy."

She surprised a bark of laughter out of him, which made her smile become a teasing grin.

"Then let's get naked again and you can take a second bite."

Without warning, he stood then scooped her up off the couch into his arms and against his chest.

Her arms looped loosely around his neck as he turned and headed in the direction of what had to be the bedroom.

As he walked, he felt her lips on his neck, quickly followed by her teeth nipping at his skin. His blood pressure spiked. So did his temperature. The combination lit his already primed body on fire. He picked up his pace and shouldered open the door in front of him. Stopping at the foot of the bed, he stopped for quick appraisal of her double-size mattress.

"You're right. I'm not gonna fit on this bed."

Her teeth lodged in his right earlobe and he shuddered at the quicksilver sensation that ran through him.

"We'll make it work."

Damn right they would. He wanted her as many times as he could get it up tonight and if he got only two hours of sleep, he could live with that. But she probably couldn't.

"What time to do you start tomorrow?" he asked.

She laughed, throwing her head back, which thrust her breasts out. And made his mouth water.

"That's what you're thinking about right now?"

"You said I was a boy scout."

"Yes, I did. I don't start until two in the afternoon. We've got some time to kill before I need to get to sleep."

He laid her on her back on the bed and planted his fists on either side of her shoulders before hovering his lips over hers. "Then let's not waste it."

FIVE

"Hey, sweetheart. Your dad said you were going to stop by tonight. Did you have dinner yet? I made pulled pork the other night. I can make you a plate."

RJ returned his mom's hug, leaning down to let her kiss his cheek and ruffle his hair. He was almost thirty-one years old, but... She was his mom.

"No, thanks. I'm good. Dad in his office? Said he wanted to talk to me."

"Yep, go on back. Just make sure you say bye before you leave."

"Of course."

His mom's smile flashed before she started back toward the family room off the kitchen.

Of course he'd never leave without saying good-bye to his mom, and Sugar's comment last night about him being a boy scout popped into his head. If she were here, she'd grin and say, "Told you."

What would his mom think of Sugar? Before the California shit, his mom had started to ask subtle questions about his future. Mainly, when was he going to find a partner and settle down. He'd always told her she'd be the first person he'd tell. At the time, he'd been dating Marisol. His parents had met her several times over the couple of years they dated, and even though his mom had never said anything bad about his ex, he'd known his mom had never warmed up to her.

He didn't think his mom outright disliked her. It was more that Marisol and his mom had nothing in common. And yeah, he knew that if he'd truly loved Marisol and had wanted to spend his life with her, it wouldn't have mattered what his mom thought.

But his mom was a damn good judge of character. And her coolness toward Marisol should've been a hint. One he probably should've heeded earlier. Because when the shit had hit the fan in L.A., she'd practically left skid marks on her way out the door. Hell, if he hadn't made an unannounced stop at his condo before practice, she would've been gone with nothing more than a good-bye text and a status update on Facebook.

His mom never would've bailed on his dad. They were equal partners in their relationship. Even though his mom hadn't worked outside the house, his dad had never made her feel like her opinion didn't matter or she didn't get a say in any decision. They always talked about everything.

RJ had realized later in life that his mom had definitely had the harder job, raising three kids and making sure her husband had the time and space needed to pursue his career and become a legendary player destined for the Hockey Hall of Fame.

Marisol had played the part of the perfect hockey girlfriend. She'd always deferred to him, no matter what. As if she didn't want to deny him anything for fear she'd piss him off. Or worse, dump her. He hadn't realized until the assault accusations had hit that she'd been more afraid of losing her star athlete boyfriend than she'd been of losing *him*. Not even a month after they'd broken up, she'd started dating an NFL player.

Sugar was Marisol's opposite in a lot of ways. And that was probably a good thing.

No probably about it.

He looked at his watch. Still an hour and a half until she got off work. Would she think he was stalking her if he went to the other restaurant she was working at tonight and waited for her to leave?

Yeah, she probably would.

Shaking his head, he headed for the stairs and took them up to his dad's office on the second floor. Their home in Chestnut Hill was small by neighborhood standards but still had four bedrooms, one of which his dad had co-opted for his office.

The door was open, his dad's head down over his desk, engrossed in the papers spread across the flat surface. RJ knocked on the frame, and his dad motioned for him to come in, still focused on the papers.

He walked up to the desk, curious to see what held his dad's interest. Not surprisingly, they were scouting sheets. The name at the top of one caught his eye. He knew the last name but the first was female. At least, he thought it was.

"Hey, is that Doug Gardiner's daughter? Is she scouting?" He pointed at the top sheet. "How's she doing?"

Doug Mitchell glanced up then pushed back in his chair with a sigh and waved his hand over the papers, as if he was performing some kind of spell. His dad was fairly new to the general manager's job, but hockey was in his blood. And he'd been a damn good player, better than either RJ or Brody would ever be.

"Yeah, it's Gard's daughter and she's fucking amazing, which I plan to tell everyone who'll listen. I have to admit I wasn't sure what to expect at first, but she's got a damn good eye. I know training camp doesn't start for a few weeks, but we've got a couple weak spots and she's—"

His dad cut off, shook his head, and chuckled. "Sorry. I didn't ask you to stop to talk shop. Or at least, not exactly. You want a beer? I could use a beer."

His dad got up and headed for the mini fridge in the fully stocked bar on the other side of the room. While RJ's mom had had full reign over the rest of the house, this room was totally Doug Mitchell. Dark-stained molding, dark blue paint. Two framed *Sports Illustrated* covers from his playing days. And a shelf that went around the entire room with pucks marked with a date, from his first professional goal to the puck from the last game he played, and every milestone in between, including every goal he scored in every Stanley Cup final. The repository of a legendary career.

RJ tried not to be intimidated every time he walked in here, but it was damn hard not to be.

His dad handed him a beer, knowing without asking what RJ would've asked for. Because his dad was good at that kind of stuff. Hell, his dad was good at everything.

"So." His dad eased back into his chair and leaned back. "I've got kind of a huge favor to ask. I don't need an answer tonight. Don't want an answer tonight. Take some time and think about it. And it's a big ask, so think carefully."

RJ shook his head, his curiosity piqued. "Okay. Now that I'm sufficiently wary, I guess I need to know what the favor is."

His dad laughed, shook his head and took a sip of his beer. "Sorry. Got a lot on my mind right now. And this...throws a wrench into a few well-laid plans."

"Then I guess you better tell me what's going on."

His dad grimaced and RJ's brows rose.

"Hey, is something wrong?"

"No, no." He leaned forward, his expression clearing a little as he leaned on his desk. "It's nothing like that. Sorry, don't mean to be cryptic. It's just...I'm kind of at a loss and if you don't say yes, I don't know what I'm going to do. But I don't want to strong-arm you into this."

"Then it must be something huge. What's up?"

"The housing I had set up for Patrick Prescott fell through."

Damn, that was a problem. Rickie Prescott was a barely eighteen-year-old phenom from a large, close-knit family in Texas, a kid whose dark skin made him one of a small number of black players in the sport and whose talent made him one of the best rookies ever. Six-foot-two, two hundred pounds and still growing, the right winger played with the heart of a true grinder.

Due to some savvy trades and maneuvering on RJ's dad's part, the Colonials had signed the kid during the first round of the draft in June. RJ's dad had immediately made plans for Rickie to attend Rookie Camp the first week of September.

Rickie would need, at most, a season in the AHL because the kid had so much natural talent, but he needed polish. The coaches wanted a look at him before he headed to the Reading Redtails, the Colonials' AHL affiliate. Rickie wasn't going to college, so he'd start the season in the fall.

But the kid's parents had been adamant that the eighteen-year-old have "adequate adult supervision." The youngest of seven, Rickie had never traveled anywhere without at least one member of his family. This summer, however, neither his older siblings nor his parents could afford to travel halfway across the country and spend a few weeks in Philly away from jobs and school. So RJ's dad had set up Rickie with the team's assistant offensive coach, who had two sons of his own only a few years younger than Rickie.

"What happened?"

"Dom's mother-in-law fell and injured herself pretty badly. Dom and his wife are already on their way to Kansas to help with the ranch and take care of her when she gets out of the hospital. But that leaves Rickie without a place to stay. At least, one that meets his parents' standards."

"Damn, that's tough. So what do you want to ask—Oh, wait." Shock zapped through him. "You want him to stay with *me*?"

His dead looked deadly serious. "I said it was a big ask."

RJ's mouth dropped open. "I would think I'm the last person you'd think of for this. And I can't imagine his parents would want him to stay with me, either."

Shaking his head, his dad let out a sigh. "RJ, anyone who has ever met you knows you would never assault a woman. The police never charged you and the guys who were guilty swore up and down you weren't there. You've gotta let this go. Besides, you were already on their approved list. You're one of the kid's idols, apparently. And I had a long conversation with his parents after he signed. They believe in you."

They believed in him? What the hell did that mean? That they trusted him with their eighteen-year-old kid?

It was on the tip of his tongue to refuse. He wasn't sure he wanted to be responsible for a kid Rickie's age. Two years ago... Yeah, he wouldn't have had a second thought. He would've been honored to be asked and thrilled to have the kid stay with him for a few weeks.

Now...

Shit.

His dad must have read his thoughts because he held up a hand just as RJ was about to open his mouth.

"Like I said, I don't need an answer now. Take the weekend to think about it. Let me know Monday. Just...think about it, okay? I'm not gonna lie. I'm worried about you, kid, and I think it'd be good for you to have something or someone else to think about."

It was useless to tell his dad he didn't need to worry because everyone knew RJ hadn't been himself since he'd come to Philly. Being accused of an assault you didn't commit tended to piss you off and make you bitter.

And even though no one he loved or who mattered to him believed he'd laid a hand on that woman, just the fact that he'd been accused still made him so angry, he got sick to his stomach. So, no, he hadn't been able to let it go completely.

"Nothing to be worried about. I'm fine."

He wasn't in danger of harming himself. No, he didn't smile as much as he used to, but he'd had his eyes opened to a few truths after the accusation. Grown a tougher skin. That wasn't necessarily a bad thing.

And last night, he'd taken the woman he'd been dreaming about for months to bed. And he was probably going to do the same again tomorrow.

So, yeah, things were better. But he'd never be the person he'd been before. His parents didn't understand that yet. Actually, none of his family or friends understood that yet.

Sugar hadn't known him before so she didn't look at him through the same lens.

His dad's expression proved RJ's point. His dad didn't think he was fine.

"Good. Glad to hear it. I still think this would be a good thing for you. Just think about it."

RJ nodded, but he was pretty sure he already knew what his answer would be.

"SO DAD finally asked you about Rickie. He told me he was going to. I stopped by the house for a few minutes this afternoon and he asked me what I thought."

Sitting at his usual table at The Brig Thursday evening, RJ

waited for his brother to continue, but Brody, being Brody, made him ask.

"Am I going to have to drag it out of you?"

Brody grinned and stole a fry off RJ's plate. "I thought you were in training. Why are you eating this shit?"

"Because I can. Brody. Are you just here to eat my food or what?"

"Actually, I'm waiting for Tara to get here."

"So you're just going to sit there and piss me off? You think it's a bad idea, right?"

Brody's eyebrows rose. "Why would I think that?"

"Because it's a bad idea."

"Bullshit. You and the kid were practically made for each other. He'll be the little brother you always wanted. Milk and cookies before bed. Up at dawn. Work out all day. Veggies for dinner."

"I have a little brother. He's an ass."

Brody snorted. "I'm not wrong. Well, maybe about the milk and cookies but everything else—"

"Look, I need some guidance here."

"No, you don't." Brody stared him down. "You know what you need to do."

"Hey, Brody. Long time, no see. How's it going?"

Brody looked up with a grin. "Hey, Sugar. It's going. What's new?"

RJ wasn't sure Brody noticed Sugar's slight pause, but RJ certainly did. It took everything RJ had not to respond in a way that would tip off Brody to the change in his relationship with Sugar.

When he'd walked through the diner entrance today after his workout, he'd been careful not to smile too much. He was acutely aware of the fact that they hadn't talked since Tuesday night. He'd gotten her number before he'd left but hadn't contacted her.

She'd said she was going to be working and he hadn't wanted to distract her. Well, actually, he *had* wanted to distract her. But he didn't.

Because he was trying not to be an asshole.

She'd acknowledged him with a nod then took an order from a table with a couple of young guys who grinned at her like hungry wolves. It'd set RJ's teeth on edge, but he'd reminded himself that they'd shared one night together. One. That didn't give him rights to any part of her time. They hadn't even had a date yet. Hell, he wasn't even sure he wanted to date right now.

Asshole.

Yep. Totally sounded like a dick move. The thought didn't sit well with him.

He'd returned her nod with what he hoped was a neutral smile and headed for his usual table. When she'd walked over to take his order, she'd treated him like she always did, her smile bright.

And he'd wanted more.

Don't be an asshole.

She'd left with another smile and not long after that, Brody had walked in. They'd talked about Brody and Tara's vacation to the Bahamas. They'd only been able to get a few days away because of Tara's work schedule. RJ had expected Brody to be grumpy about that. Brody's default mood was grumpy. But Tara had a calming effect on the guy. Amazing.

And after Sugar had dropped off his dinner, along with an extra side of steamed broccoli and carrots he hadn't ordered, he forced his attention back to his brother and his dilemma about Rickie. He'd expected Brody to agree that putting Rickie with him was a bad idea.

"Nothing much," Sugar answered Brody's question, pulling RJ out of his thoughts. "How was your trip?"

"Great. Nice just to lie on a beach with nothing to do. I keep telling this guy he needs to get away, but he doesn't listen to me. Sun, sand, and someone to share it with. You gotta get out more. Or you're never gonna get laid again."

RJ couldn't help it. He looked up at Sugar, whose cheeks had turned bright red.

Without thinking about it, RJ kicked Brody under the table, hard enough that his brother swore under his breath.

"What the fu—" Then Brody looked up at Sugar. "Shit, sorry, Shug. I'm a cretin, or so my sister likes to call me. But I'm the one with the girlfriend, so..."

RJ was going to punch his brother. Just a little pop on the nose.

Sugar roused herself a split second later, carefully keeping her attention on Brody.

"You're not a cretin. Trust me. I've known a few. And I think you're right." She looked straight into RJ's eyes, a definite challenge there. "I think RJ needs a vacation. He pushes himself way too hard. Now, you want to order something, or you want to wait 'til Tara gets here?"

"See," Brody nodded at RJ, "I'm not the only one." He looked back up at Sugar with a conspiratorial grin. "I'll wait for Tara. Thanks."

"You got it. Everything okay, RJ?"

No, not really.

"It's all good. Thanks, Sugar."

Did her smile look a little different? A hint of heat from the other night? Or was he seeing something that wasn't there?

He tore his gaze away as she walked off. And met his brother's gaze head-on.

"Something going on you wanna talk about?"

RJ took a second to think about his answer because Brody looked intent. Brody had never been known for being observant.

Before Tara had come along, Brody was more likely to ignore a potential emotional situation than approach it head-on. Before he and Tara had hooked up, Brody probably would've been oblivious to any undercurrents between RJ and Sugar.

Now, he sat there looking at RJ like he expected him to spill his guts. He considered several responses and settled on the easiest.

"No. Why?"

Brody's eyes narrowed and his head tilted just a little to the side.

Should've kept it at no.

"Let me rephrase the question. Is there something going on between you and Sugar?"

Damn it. RJ didn't want to lie to his brother. He also didn't want to face an inquisition either. So he kept his mouth shut. Which basically gave Brody the answer he was looking for.

"Huh." Brody nodded, just once, like he was putting a period on a statement. And maybe he was. "I did *not* see that one coming."

"Brody—"

"Dude, I'm not here to give you shit. I like Sugar. A lot. I think she's amazing. I also think your head's still fucked up, and I don't want to see either of you get hurt."

"Who are you and what did you do with my brother?"

Brody gave him the finger like he should've expected it.

"And now you're deflecting. Interesting."

It took all of RJ's control not to show any outward sign of discomfort. "There's nothing to tell. At least nothing I want to talk about. I'm still allowed to have a private life, right?"

Brody shrugged. "I don't know. I mean, do you still remember *how* to have a private life? Because you haven't had one for months. Which is part of the reason Dad is pairing you up with Rickie. You realize that, right? He's worried about you."

Sighing, RJ shook his head. "No one needs to be worried about me. I'm fine. Maybe I'm just not the same person I was before all that shit happened in L.A. Maybe I just need some fucking space."

Brody's brows rose and RJ wanted to take back the words as soon as they left his lips. Because he didn't use that word as casually as some people. Not unless he was really pissed off.

Or frustrated. Or just messed up in the head, apparently.

"Damn it, Brody. Don't—"

"Hey, man, I'm sorry. I didn't mean to push."

"Is everything...okay?"

Sugar stood by their table again, but this time, she wasn't wearing a smile, and he had to wonder if she'd heard him.

"Yeah, we're fine, Shug." Brody gave her an easy smile. "Just pushed a few of the old man's buttons."

RJ gave Brody a look that promised retribution before he turned his full attention to Sugar. Her lips no longer wore an easy smile and her eyes held questions.

Shit. Had she heard him? Did she think he was talking about her?

Hell, right now, she was one person he didn't want to give him space.

"Sure." She flashed a smile at Brody, but it didn't have its usual brightness. "Just let me know if you need anything else."

She walked away again, and this time, he let his gaze follow her before looking back at Brody.

Brody's half-assed grin returned. "Still wanna tell me there's nothing going on there?"

"I'm not telling you anything. Let it go."

"Does anyone else know?"

When RJ didn't answer, Brody nodded.

"Okay, it'll be our secret. But you know when Tara gets

here, you're gonna need to get better at keeping your mental pants zipped, if you know what I mean."

The statement was so ridiculous, RJ couldn't help but laugh, shaking his head the whole time.

"Seriously, though." Brody's expression was all business now. "If you want to keep your private life private, I totally get it. I've been where you are. But you know Janine and Georgie are gonna pick up on whatever's going on with you two. They consider Sugar family. You hurt her and you're gonna be *persona non grata* around here."

"Jesus, Brody, I'm not asking her to marry me. We're just..."

When he couldn't come up with the appropriate word, Brody helped him out.

"Screwing around?"

RJ really didn't like that phrase, probably because "screwing around" indicated a lack of feeling. And RJ had a mess of feelings for Sugar. Most of which involved the two of them together and naked. But not just because he wanted to have sex with her.

"No. That's not it."

"I know that." Brody's voice held no trace of doubt. "I just wanted to make sure you did too."

SIX

By the time ten o'clock rolled around, Sugar's feet throbbed, her calves ached, and her stomach had a knot in it that wouldn't untangle.

Brody and Tara had left an hour ago, after Tara had hurried in long enough to gulp down a salad. Sugar liked Tara. She was smart, said what she wanted to say, and loved Brody to distraction. Lucky for her, because Brody, though he wasn't an overly demonstrative kind of guy, made sure Tara knew he loved her back.

RJ was still in his booth. That wasn't unusual, except that, after last night, nothing seemed usual with him now. Everything he said, every look he gave her, made her hyperaware of him. Considering how they'd spent last night, it made sense. But it was the little piece of conversation she'd caught between the brothers that'd made that knot tighten even more.

She knew it was stupid to get worked up over a conversation she'd only heard part of, but she'd let it get to her anyway. Had he been talking about her when he'd said he needed space? They'd spent one night together and had made no plans to see each other again. Except here he was today. At his usual table, reading a book and drinking coffee.

He'd smiled every time she'd arrived to refresh his mug, a smile she was becoming to think of as hers. And that was dangerous. So dangerous.

Since it was so close to closing, she was making one last round of the tables, which included a couple on the other side of the room, who refused more coffee and got up to pay, leaving her alone with RJ.

Georgie was busy in the back, cleaning the kitchen, so she wasn't there to see Sugar hesitate before going back to RJ, who watched her approach with a look she'd couldn't figure out.

So instead of gnawing at it mentally, she figured what the hell. Might as well just ask.

"Is everything okay?"

He responded after a split-second pause, which may just have been her imagination. Or not.

"Yes. Would you like to come back to my place tonight when you're done?"

Her immediate response was a giddy desire to say yes. But she should set some ground rules first, right? Or at least ask him what his intentions were? Which was ridiculous because this was only the second time he'd asked her out.

And really, the first didn't count because she'd asked him back to her apartment and that was all the further they'd gotten.

She'd been planning to do some schoolwork tonight because her weekend was full of work. She had that split double tomorrow then she was working ten hours Saturday until two in the morning and another ten on Sunday but only until nine. She'd planned to do her wash Sunday night so she could take her books to the basement with her and study then.

"Yeah, I would."

He didn't crack a smile, but he nodded, and that intensity

was back in his eyes. So she guessed he was happy with her answer.

"Good."

"I need to shower first. Can I meet you there?"

She was almost afraid he was going to say forget it, but RJ just nodded and slid out of the booth to stand next to her. "I'll text you my address and give the doorman your name. He'll send you up. See you in a half hour."

RJ'S BUILDING was only a few blocks away, so Sugar decided to walk rather than get a taxi or Uber. She hoped the walk would help work out some of her nerves.

It took her fifteen minutes to shower and dry her hair, put on a little makeup, and obsess over what to wear. If tonight went like Tuesday night, she wouldn't be wearing it long, so what did it really matter?

She was still wearing a smile when she grabbed a pretty pink-and-white-striped sundress out of her closet then pulled out a pair of flat sandals that were cute but wouldn't hurt her feet on the walk. Not exactly sexy, but hopefully he wouldn't be looking at her feet.

And luckily, it wasn't that hot, so she shouldn't be sweating like a pig by the time she got there.

Stepping out onto the sidewalk, she breathed a little sigh of relief that even in the middle of summer, there were still lots of people out walking. The small town nearest her parents' home had rolled up its sidewalks by seven o'clock at night, and if you happened to be caught on the streets after that, half the town wanted to know if you were lost and the other half figured you were up to no good and called your parents.

It'd been one of the main reasons she couldn't wait to move

away. Of course, a big city like Philly had its own problems. She had a can of pepper spray and a panic button dangling from her purse and within easy reach. She'd never had to use them, but she'd reached for them a few times when a guy had gotten a little too close.

Tonight, a few guys gave her a second look, but she was moving at a pace that discouraged anyone from even whistling at her. If they had... Hell, she probably wouldn't have noticed anyway.

When she finally got to RJ's building, she stopped outside to make sure she had the right address because, wow. Maybe she should've called for a ride and worn heels. A building like this definitely deserved heels.

It was old but not out-of-date. In fact, it looked like it'd been renovated recently. As she stepped inside the lobby, she could tell it was cleaned every day. She faintly smelled sandalwood and not a whiff of disinfectant. The marble security desk sparkled, and the forty-something doorman wore dress slacks and a crisp white shirt with the name of the building embroidered on the chest pocket.

He gave her a discreet head-to-toe then nodded. "Can I help you?"

Okay, not the most pleasant guy in the world.

"Hi there." She pulled out a bright smile. "I'm here to see RJ Mitchell."

The guy's expression changed so subtly, she almost believed she imagined it, and now his lips curved in a little bit of a smile. She knew that if she'd shown up unannounced and asked for RJ, he would be escorting her back out the door to the sidewalk.

No, she didn't look like she belonged in this fancy-ass building. She wasn't wearing a thousand-dollar dress and four-inch stiletto heels. Then again, she didn't look like she lived on the street either.

Maybe you have a little chip on your shoulder, missy.

And there was her mom's voice, just in the nick of time to make her feel completely insignificant.

"Your name?"

"Sugar Donahue."

He didn't bother to check his screen or tablet or wherever he kept the list of approved guests, just pointed to the bank of elevators to the left of the desk.

"You can go up. Tenth floor."

Smiling a little wider than she normally would have, Sugar said, "Thank you," and headed in that direction with an extra swing in her hips. Just because she could.

The elevator opened almost immediately, and she walked into the spacious, mirrored box that rivaled the size of her bathroom. Okay, that was stretching it, but still.

Trying not to be ridiculously overwhelmed, Sugar punched the "10" button and took a deep breath, fighting a case of nerves that seemed to rise out of nowhere. Which pissed her off. She didn't have one damn thing to be embarrassed or ashamed about. And anyone who thought otherwise could take a long walk off a short pier.

Maybe you're reading too much into a look.

Yeah, maybe. Okay, probably. But even though her parents had money, she hadn't been raised like an heiress. She'd been raised on a farm in the middle of nowhere where she'd been the primary caregiver for her four younger sisters.

Okay, maybe she did have a little bit of a chip on her shoulders. She'd sworn when she moved out, she was going to take care of herself first, at least until she found a partner worthy of her. Because, damn it, she deserved one.

Was RJ the guy? He might be. Or he could still turn out to be a douche, though she really didn't think that was going to happen now. She hoped.

Oh hell, was she really trying to talk herself out of this?

No. She really wasn't.

The bell dinged and the doors opened, and she realized she'd barely noticed the elevator moving. Walking out, she stopped to check the silver plaque on the wall with numbers and arrows then made her way down the hall. For the size of the building, there didn't seem to be enough doors.

Shaking her head at her scattered thoughts, she found RJ's door and knocked before she talked herself out of it. Two seconds later, it opened, and she found herself forgetting every thought in her head as she stared up into RJ's eyes.

He smiled, and her heart flipped over in her chest. Hell, it wasn't even one of his all-out grins, but it still made her want to strip off all his clothes and throw herself at him.

What would he do if she just grabbed his pants and started to unbutton them?

He probably wouldn't say no, because what guy would, right?

"Hey. Come on in. I'm glad you're here."

He waved her inside and she stepped into an apartment that didn't look like RJ even lived here. Or that anyone lived here.

"Thanks for inviting me. Did you just move in? Everything's so...perfect. Or you have a damn good housekeeper."

He laughed as he closed the door, a low, husky sound that made her nipples peak.

"I do have a really good cleaning service." He closed the door and stepped up next to her. "But mainly, I just haven't had a lot of time to decorate. And honestly, I haven't really thought about it much. My mom and sister say the same thing. Of course, my dad and Brody have never said a word about it so..."

She smiled up at him, realizing he was making an effort at small talk, trying to put her at ease. Because even though she didn't want to admit it, she was a little keyed up and he must've clued into that.

"Was it tough? Picking up and moving across the country? Uprooting your whole life?"

He didn't answer right away, and she wondered if she'd overstepped. But honestly, how could she be overstepping after the amazing sex they'd had?

"Yeah, it was. You want something to drink?"

Okay, guess she could take a hint. He didn't want to talk about something so personal. Got it.

"Sure."

"Beer, lemonade, or soda? Not really a wine guy, sorry."

"And I'm not really a wine girl, so you're good. Lemonade would be great."

His smile was back, this time a little easier, and she wondered if maybe he was feeling a little awkward, too. Probably not. She couldn't think of any reason why he would. This was his ground, his turf.

"Come on into the kitchen with me. You hungry? I'm not much of a cook, but I'm pretty good at turning on the microwave."

And just like that, she realized how easy it would be fall in love with this guy. And boy would that be one hell of a problem. Because RJ seemed dead set against getting close to anyone.

DAMN IT, don't be an ass. You can't invite her over then hustle her into bed as soon as she crosses the threshold.

Which was exactly what he wanted to do. Luckily, he knew better and restrained himself. But, from the second she'd walked in, he'd known he'd do anything to keep her here tonight, short of restraints and kidnapping, of course. Unless she was into the restraints, then he had enough ties they could make do. And that probably wasn't what he should be thinking about either.

So, before he shoved his foot in his mouth and said something ridiculous, he led her into the kitchen to get her a glass of lemonade and a beer for himself so he had something to do with his hands. Which he wanted to put all over her.

She looked beautiful. And sexy. He wanted to put his fingers under the dress straps and pull them down her shoulders. Then he'd tug on the little string around her waist and let the dress drop to the floor. He was dying to see whatever she was wearing underneath.

But he also didn't want to rush. She was here. And if he played his cards right, she'd stay all night.

"Wow, what a great kitchen. Do you use it at all?"

Her voice held a note of wonder that made him look around the room as he handed her a glass before going back inside the fridge for his beer. This kitchen was smaller than the one in California, which Marisol had always complained about being too tiny.

"Not really, no. I can make a mean grilled cheese or an omelet. But I can't honestly remember the last time I used the oven. Does that make me less interesting?"

Her laughter filled the room and when she shook her head, her hair flowed over her shoulders and down her back. "Not at all. I need to be able to do something better than you, and I've picked up a few tricks at the diner. But boy, I would love to cook in here."

"Any time you want. Although don't take that as me asking you to cook for me. I can also make one hell of a club sandwich."

"Now that sounds good. Let me give you a hand."

As if they'd broken through some invisible uneasy cloud, he relaxed. He hadn't realized how tense he'd been until his shoulders released. They moved around the kitchen as he told her where to find the bread while he pulled everything he needed out of the fridge.

Their conversation stuck to easy stuff. Mayo or mustard. Rye bread or wheat. Good thing he'd had groceries delivered yesterday. Before his dad had asked him about taking in Rickie.

"RJ? Something wrong?"

He realized he was about to ruin his sandwich by putting mustard on his toast. Luckily, he'd already put hers on a plate and she was in the middle of piling it with lunch meat.

"No, sorry. It's just...my dad asked me for a favor last night and I'm not sure what to do about it."

"I guess it depends on the favor. My parents never asked me if I wanted to do anything. They usually just said 'Here' and put a kid in my lap or gave me money to get groceries."

"Sounds like they relied on you for a lot."

She shrugged. "If you mean used me to keep the kids out of their hair and to keep them fed, then, yeah, they did. So, what does your dad want you to do?"

He'd much rather talk about her, but she'd asked so... "He wants me to take in a rookie for a week during camp."

After cutting their sandwiches in half-triangles, like she probably did at the diner a hundred times a day, she climbed onto one of the chairs at the island and took a bite of her roast beef and swiss. He took the seat next to her, close enough that their knees could touch.

He hoped he'd be touching a lot more than her knees tonight. And since she'd agreed to come over, he was optimistic he was going to get what he wanted. Sugar in his bed.

"Do you know him already?"

"No. But everything I've heard about him is good."

"How young is he?"

"Just turned eighteen."

Her lips twitched and he saw laughter lurking in her eyes.

Frowning slightly, he lowered his sandwich before asking, "What's so funny?"

"You say that like you're ancient."

"Some days I feel like it."

"You're only thirty-one."

He shrugged. "I've traveled a lot of miles between eighteen and thirty-one."

Sometimes he felt like he still had a lot of road ahead of him, but then he considered the fact that his best friend had retired from playing at the end of last season. Tank had hung up his skates and was settling into a goalie coach position with the Reading Redtails, the Colonials' AHL affiliate. So far, he seemed to like it.

"How long do you think you'll play?"

It sounded like such an offhand question, one that didn't require a lot of thought. But for RJ, it did. Probably because he overthought everything lately.

"I've been thinking about that a lot."

Sugar's head tilted to the side, her eyes narrowing as she studied him. She chewed, swallowed, and set her sandwich on the plate before propping her chin on one hand and looking deeply into his eyes.

"Sounds like you're thinking about making a change. Don't you want to play anymore?"

"It's not that. I still love to play." Mostly. "It's just..."

Just what?

She didn't say the words, but he clearly saw her question in the arch of her eyebrows.

"It's been tough to find the joy I once had in the game."

She shrugged, like he wasn't saying anything she hadn't heard before. "You're not a kid anymore. Kids think everything is bright and shiny and fun. Adults realize work is work. You can love what you do and still think it's a burden. My mom used to say, if you love what you do, you'll never work a day in your life. That's straight-up bullshit. It's still work. You still have to make sure you're doing it right. You just need to make sure you're doing it for the right reasons."

Damn, she fascinated him. "And what are the right reasons?"

"You have to please yourself first. You will never make everyone happy, but if you can't make yourself happy, you will be miserable for damn sure."

"You've got it all worked out, don't you?"

She laughed, covering her mouth with her hand because she'd just taken a bite of food.

"Oh god. I wish. There are days I wish I hadn't left the farm. It would've been easier, just to stay. My dad offered to pay for college if I stayed home another couple of years. But there was no way in hell I wasn't leaving. I mean, I didn't leave right away. My youngest sister was pretty attached to me, so I hung around for a couple years. Worked around town, saved up everything I could, and finally got the hell out."

She said that last part so forcefully, he had to wonder if there was more to her story than she was saying. Another guy might've avoided the hell out of that conversation, especially if he wanted to get laid. RJ wanted to know everything about her.

"So did you move to Philly right away?"

She looked down, breaking the connection between them. Hiding something under the guise of picking up her sandwich.

"No. I moved in with my boyfriend for a while."

Wait. A boyfriend? She'd never mentioned—

"Until he died."

Whoa. Okay. Hadn't been expecting that.

"What happened?"

She looked up and her eyes were sad, her smile bittersweet. "Suicide. He struggled with depression all through high school, but we thought he was doing better after we graduated. He worked on his family's farm and we talked about moving away. And then one day… He took an entire bottle of his dad's fentanyl. Then he walked into the pond and let himself drown. His parents still think it was a freak accident. That the amount of fentanyl in his system was too high to be real. I think he deliberately took it by the pond and let himself drown so everyone would think that's what happened. That maybe they wouldn't do a tox screen, you know? That maybe he wouldn't cause his parents so much pain."

"Damn, Sugar. I'm sorry. That had to be awful. How old was he?"

"Nineteen. He would've been twenty-three next month."

"I'm really sorry."

"Thanks." She nodded, smiling at him. "It seems like forever ago. But sometimes something'll happen, and I think, 'I gotta call Bobby. He'd get such a laugh out of this.' And then I remember."

"Is that when you moved to Philly?"

Another nod. "I'd been looking for apartments we could afford but that'd been based on both of us working and sharing expenses. So instead I rented a room in a basement in South Philly and got a job working for tips at a bar down the street. Two years ago, I walked into The Brig because they had a sign in the window and I never left."

Her smile made his heart skip a few beats.

"Georgie and Janine have a way of doing that to people. You walk in one day because someone says they have the best meatloaf in the city and the next day you're telling Georgie your deepest secrets."

Laughing now, Sugar let her head fall back for a few seconds. "Yeah, she has that effect on people. I'm just glad I found them when I did. I was ready to give up and go home."

"I'm glad you didn't."

She nodded, her smile disappearing but the warmth in her eyes getting hotter. "Me too."

They finished their sandwiches then, keeping the conversation light and away from talk of suicide and accusations of assault. He found himself listening more than talking, which was unusual for him. At least, it had been. Lately, he'd found himself without much to say. Everyone who knew him had noticed and had tried to get him to engage more. Which just made him shut down even more.

Sugar didn't seem to have a problem with him being quiet. And with her, it wasn't hard to find his voice. He'd half expected awkward pauses and uncomfortable silences. Then again, he should've known better, because Sugar had never met a stranger.

By the time they'd finished eating, he knew she preferred Springsteen to Lennon, watched enough crime shows to get away with murder, and would much rather study than listen to a professor drone away. A few minutes ago, he'd asked her if she'd ever traveled and that had set them off on a fifteen-minute conversation about where they'd like to visit.

"You've *actually* been to Russia? Was it weird? I've never even thought about going there. I mean, I'm sure it's really cool, but someday I want to go to Greece and Italy. All those ruins and museums and beaches and it's *warm*. I mean, it's warm here too, but I want to see the Mediterranean. It must be so beautiful."

"It is. My, ah, well, I spent a couple weeks in Capri last year. My former girlfriend had family there, so we went to visit and do some sightseeing. One of the most amazing places I've ever been. And the food is incredible."

"Yes! If I ever get there, I will eat myself into a coma, I just know it. Did you have a bad breakup?"

Since he'd left himself open to the question by bringing up Marisol, he'd expected her question.

"Not really, no. She stuck around a few days, told everyone she totally believed I was innocent, then bailed for a pro football player."

"Whoa. Total bitch."

He shrugged. "No. Just...shallow."

He'd never allowed himself to say that out loud before. It felt good.

"Oh, definitely shallow. But also a bitch."

His grin widened, which made her shake her head.

"I'm sorry. I know I shouldn't—"

"Don't apologize. It's nothing my sister hasn't said a hundred times."

"I knew I liked Gabby. And Tara. And the more I get to know Brody, the more I like him."

That made him laugh. "Yeah, Brody can take a little time to warm up to."

"Oh, I don't think he's a dick or anything. I just don't know him that well and he can come off a little..."

She bit her lip, her brow furrowed, clearly trying to come up with something to say about his brother that wouldn't hurt his feelings.

"Like a dick?" he said.

Her nose wrinkled as she slid off the stool and grabbed their plates before he had a chance to tell her to leave them.

"No. And lately, he's been a lot more open. Probably because of Tara."

"Definitely because of Tara. She's good for him."

"Yeah." She opened the dishwasher and put their plates inside, taking the glasses from his hand and putting them in, as well. As if they'd done this a thousand times. "I think so too. He's been much easier to talk to lately."

"Easier than me?"

"Sometimes." She leaned back against the counter, arms crossed over her chest. "Sometimes, you seem really angry."

His brows arched in surprise before he could hide it. "What makes you think that?"

"Because I watch you." Her shoulders lifted and her gaze didn't meet his. "I mean, we haven't known each other long, but I know your brother and Tank are worried about you, so obviously, you're different than they remember you."

He moved closer, until he stood only inches away. Close enough to smell the vanilla scent of her hair. His fingers itched to wrap themselves in the silky strands.

"Have they told you that?"

He didn't know if it was the low tone of his voice or his nearness, but she swallowed hard and straightened a little, as if she'd realized he was much closer than she'd expected. Or maybe she just wanted to be ready...for whatever came next.

Shaking her head, she wove her hand through her hair to push it back over her shoulder. His mouth watered to taste the bare skin just above her breasts.

"No, of course not." Her tone said it was a ridiculous question. "They love you. They're not going to talk about you to the diner waitress."

"Maybe I'm not the same person I was before. Maybe my family just don't like who I've become."

"Who do you think you are now?"

"I think I'm the man who's trying not to strip you naked right now and fuck you in the kitchen."

Her smile was immediate as she reached for his waist and pulled him into her body.

"I'm sure your bed's more comfortable than mine. We could—"

He gripped her by the neck and kissed her hard, crushing

his lips against hers until she opened her mouth to his insistent tongue.

LUST BLASTED THROUGH SUGAR, scouring her veins with heat and making her melt against RJ like butter on the grill. Her arms wrapped around his neck, fingers sinking into his hair as she absorbed the feel of all that hard muscle straining against her.

It was a heady feeling, knowing he wanted her as much as she wanted him. All day, she'd had butterflies in her stomach, hoping to see him. She hadn't been sure if he'd show up or if, now that they'd slept together, he'd ignore her.

He definitely wasn't ignoring her. She had his complete attention, which was both thrilling and a little overwhelming. He kissed her with single-minded focus, coaxing a response that threatened to steal her breath and her ability to think rationally.

She was pretty sure all brain function was overrated right now, anyway. Especially when his hands slipped to her shoulders and pushed down the straps of her dress. Since they were the only thing holding it in place, the top slid down just enough for her breasts to be bared almost to her nipples. As if he had some sixth sense, he pulled back and looked down.

"Put your arms down."

She'd forgotten she still had them wrapped around his shoulders. Without hesitation, she did what he'd asked, and the dress slid to the floor with a whisper of sound. She hadn't worn a bra and her panties were little more than two thin cords connecting the pink lace triangle in the front to the sheer panel barely covering her ass in the back.

"Jesus, Sugar. You're going to give me a heart attack. Push those down 'cause if I do it, they're gonna get ripped."

She shivered at the raw need in his voice and wanted to say something, anything, in response. Instead, she lifted her hands to her hips, slid her thumbs into the strings at her sides then wiggled a little until she had them over her hips.

"You have a thing for watching women undress, don't you?"

His gaze snagged hers. "Only you."

She flashed hot and was sure her cheeks were summer-sunburn red. He sounded so sincere and so horny at the same time. It was a strange combination that served to melt her heart and her pussy at the same time.

"Good."

She barely heard her own reply, but he obviously did because he grinned and reached for her.

Cupping her breasts, he played with her nipples, his thumbs and forefingers pinching and rolling while he watched her face. The sensation was so intense, her pussy clenched, an orgasm already within reach. He played with her breasts for what had to be minutes, making her super-sensitive until he leaned forward and kissed her again.

This time, she thought she'd be ready, but she wasn't. She barely had enough time to suck in air before she felt his hands slid down to her hips then felt one weave through the hair on her pussy to reach her entrance. Moaning into his mouth, she rose onto her toes when he slid two fingers inside. He worked his fingers high inside her, stroking her until she thought she'd lose her mind. Her body hung on the edge of climax. She needed him to touch her clit, but he purposely kept his distance.

She tried to pull away to tell him what she wanted. He followed her, bending her back until he wrapped his other arm around her waist to hold her steady. She almost felt like struggling but it certainly wouldn't be to get away.

No, she wanted more. Needed more.

Then she remembered her hands were free. Right now, they

were clenched in the t-shirt stretched across his chest. Loosening her grip took some effort but, finally, she released the fabric and shoved her hands into the elastic waistband of his nylon shorts. If she'd been able to look, she'd be sure they hid nothing. She felt the heat of his erection the second her fingers made contact with the fabric. Drawn to it, she wrapped one hand around the shaft and cupped his balls in the other. And was rewarded with his groan.

In the next second, he slid his fingers free and lifted her off the floor. She had to release him or risk hurting him. They didn't go far or so she thought. She wasn't really sure because she was pressing open-mouthed kisses across his chest and neck and jaw, nipping at his chin before nuzzling her nose against his skin.

Seconds later, he stopped, and she figured he'd taken her to the bedroom, but she opened her eyes and realized—

"Open the medicine cabinet."

She turned her head and did as he'd told her, getting a quick impression of a spacious room with dark walls and marble countertops before fixating on the medicine cabinet. She knew what he wanted her to get and spied the condoms on the top shelf.

Plucking one from the box, she turned to look back at him but found herself sitting on the bathroom counter. The marble was cool beneath her ass, but RJ was already on his way to his knees.

Before her brain had time to catch up, he'd spread her thighs with his broad shoulders and put his mouth on her pussy. Her breath caught in her throat and she bowed forward as pure ecstasy raced through her veins. His lips and tongue worked together to bring her orgasm closer and closer but never pushing her over the edge.

She realized at that moment that she'd never been with a guy who knew how to make a woman beg. She thought she'd had good sex before but... Oh my god. She'd never had sex like this.

Moaning, she grabbed hold of the edge of the counter with both hands and let her back arch until her shoulders hit the mirror on the wall. With her eyes closed, every sensation was heightened. Every swipe of his tongue against her clit, every time he sucked on her lower lips with his mouth, every time he backed off to nip at the sensitive skin of her thighs with his teeth, she wanted to scream.

He kept pushing her, kept revving her higher, but he didn't let her come. She could feel her orgasm simmering, building, curling through her stomach and making everything tight.

Finally, she grabbed his hair and tugged, hard. She needed his attention, needed him to give her more. Instead, she swore she felt him smile against her pussy and speared his tongue between her lips. It just made her even more aware of how empty she was. How she needed to be filled.

When she was panting and fairly certain she was going to hyperventilate from delayed gratification, he stood and made her cry out in complete and utter frustration.

Her eyes flew open to find him yanking his shirt over his head with one hand and pushing his shorts down with the other. He took the condom out of her hand, which she'd forgotten she was holding, ripped it open, and rolled it down his cock.

"Look at me, Sugar."

"I am."

Her gaze was glued to the sight of his cock in his hand, as he angled it away from his body and pointed it straight at hers.

"No, Sugar. Into my eyes."

It took an effort, but she tore her attention away from what she wanted and promptly got lost in that navy-blue gaze.

"Don't look away. I want to see you when I get inside you."

She barely had time to suck in a breath at the sheer eroticism of that statement when he stepped closer, lodging the tip of his cock between her pussy lips. The blunt thickness made her pussy clench tighter in anticipation.

Waiting was hell. Wanting was a fever in her blood. Because of her position, she couldn't move, had to wait for him.

Finally, *finally*, he did, and it was everything she could have wanted.

Her lungs sucked in air as he gripped her hips and tilted her pelvis to just the right angle for his cock to slide inside. His head descended and his teeth worried the tip of one nipple as his erection lodged deep in her body. They were both breathing like they'd just climbed Everest when his hips met hers. Her legs felt stretched so wide, the burn was almost painful. It only heightened the pleasure.

She latched her hands onto his shoulders and held on for the ride.

He started slow and steady, her pussy tight but wet and so damn needy. She clung to him, making him swear.

"You feel so goddamn amazing." His voice rasped in her ear as he licked his way up her throat to nuzzle his nose into her hair. "I want to spend all night inside you."

"I'm not going anywhere," she managed to say, though she could barely breathe.

"Damn right." He pulled back, his cock almost slipping from her body before shoving back inside, this time with a little more force than before.

Her heart pounding, she clung to him as he increased the speed of his thrusts, until the base of his cock hit her clit at just the right spot. Her eyes closed as she convulsed around him, her lungs stuttering for air.

Seconds later, she heard him groan as he thrust one more time then held deep, pulsing and extending her climax until she was pretty sure she was going to pass out, it was that good.

They stayed like that for long seconds that stretched into forever.

Finally, his heavy breathing in her ear, he lifted her off the counter, his cock sliding out of her body as he shifted her into his arms.

"I swear, we're going to do this in a bed that's big enough for both of us at least once tonight."

She burst out laughing at his wry statement, letting her head fall back until she could look into his eyes.

"I don't care where we do it. I just hope you're not planning to sleep tonight."

His smile kindled something that wasn't lust but something sweeter.

"Sleep is overrated."

SEVEN

Hey Sissy! You home? Let me in!

Her sister's text barely seconds old, Sugar swung open the door Monday morning, a smile spreading across her face.

Cookie was number three of five on the Donahue menu, as their dad liked to say. Sugar, being the oldest, followed by Candy, Cookie, Honey, and Taffy. Yes, those *were* their real names because, of course, that's exactly what two wanna-be hippies would name their five daughters.

"Hey, what are you—Oh, Cookie. Seriously?"

"Surprise?!"

With a rueful smile on her face, Cookie put her hands on her huge belly and patted the mound that could only mean one thing.

Her nineteen-year-old sister was knocked up.

"Jesus, Cookie. What the hell happened?"

"Well, I'm pretty sure you know how it happened."

As she waved her sister through the door, Sugar had already started making calculations. The last time she'd seen Cookie had been six months ago. She'd come to visit before heading back to college. Her sister had to be at least eight months pregnant. Knowing Cookie, her due date was probably next week.

Biting back a sigh because she'd heard the tremble in her sister's voice, Sugar took a few seconds to close and lock the door. And take a deep breath before she hyperventilated.

Focus. No need to freak out. Yet.

Sugar took another deep breath and hoped like hell she'd wiped all trace of the need to scream off her face.

"You're right." She turned to face her sister, who'd made her way to the couch and was in the process of lowering herself onto it. "Stupid question. Let me ask another one. Is there a father in the picture?"

"There was until about two days ago."

Now tears formed in her sister's eyes, and Sugar felt the weight of the world drop onto her shoulders. Because if there was one thing Sugar knew, when her sisters needed help, they didn't go to their parents. They came to her.

The five of them had learned that lesson early. Their parents had perfected the art of hands-off parenting. Their mom had claimed Sugar came out of the womb with an old soul. By the age of ten, Sugar had figured out that was an excuse for her parents to hand over the care of her younger sisters to her. Sugar loved her parents and never doubted their love for their children, but they were never going to be candidates for parents of the year.

Sugar had been the one to get her sisters up for school and make breakfast before getting everyone on the bus and making sure they had lunch money or that Taffy had a bag lunch because of her food allergies.

It'd been Sugar who bandaged her sisters' skinned knees and combed the tangles out of their hair after they'd run wild all summer. It'd been Sugar who'd driven Honey to the emergency room when she'd fallen and broken her arm. And when she'd finally decided to leave home two years ago, it'd been Sugar who'd bawled herself to sleep the first few nights in the city, alone and hating it, but mostly hating that she hated it because it'd been all she'd dreamed about for years.

Shit. Shit. Shit. "Who—"

"I missed you. I was afraid to tell you because I know you're disappointed but I was on the pill so I never thought..."

Her sister's voice held the threat of tears. Sugar closed her eyes and admitted defeat. Hell, there hadn't even been a fight and Sugar had lost it anyway. With a sigh, Sugar sank onto the couch next to Cookie. Immediately, her sister laid her head on her shoulder and grabbed Sugar's hand.

"Please tell me you're still on Mom and Dad's health insurance."

Cookie hiccupped out a laugh and, for the life of her, Sugar couldn't understand why.

"God, I missed you, Shug. I'm sorry to show up like this. I just didn't have anywhere else to go and I couldn't go home. Mom and Dad barely raised us."

"But are you still on their health insurance?"

"Yes."

Thank God. One problem solved. At least a thousand more to go. "Have you told them? How long have you known? Why didn't you tell me? I mean, you're what? Eight months pregnant?"

Cookie touched her nose with her forefinger. "I'm due in September. And no. They don't know. I haven't been home in months. I just don't think I could deal with them right now. Mom would freak out and Dad would have a heart attack before he decided he couldn't handle it and disappeared into the barn for days."

Sugar swallowed a groan, knowing her sister was right but wishing she wasn't. "Have you been to a doctor? Where have you been living? And why the *hell* am I just now finding out you're pregnant?"

Cookie's face crinkled. "I didn't know until about three months ago. My period's always been wonky and, at first, I just thought I was gaining weight. I didn't have morning sickness, just a few days that I felt kind of off. When I realized that fluttering in my stomach wasn't gas, I was living with Jamie in Wilkes-Barre, and I just...didn't want anyone to know. I thought...I don't know, if I didn't talk about it, it would just work itself out, right? Jamie was cool at first, talking about how we'd make it work. Then about a week ago, he said he was moving to Florida for a job, and he wouldn't have room for me or a kid and I should go home. He said he'd send money."

Yeah, right. "Asshole." She could never imagine RJ doing something so vile.

"I guess." Cookie's shoulder moved against hers in a shrug. "I'm more pissed at myself that I didn't see it coming. I thought he was the one. Until...well, this."

She rubbed her belly, drawing Sugar's attention. Sweet jumping Jesus, as Anika would occasionally say. There was so much to consider right now that Sugar's brain kept short-circuiting on everything else but the fact that her younger sister was going to have a baby in a few weeks.

Her apartment only had one bedroom, but Sugar could sleep on the couch for now. Until they found someplace they could afford with two bedrooms. And they'd need a crib. And clothes. And food.

Sugar had some money put away that'd been earmarked for college, but she could dip into that.

Guess I'm not quitting that job at Nero's anytime soon.

And there was no way she could even think about starting a new job now. She had to tell RJ she wasn't interested in that job at the ice complex.

If you tell him you need help, you know he'll do whatever you need.

Wouldn't it be wonderful to have someone take over right about now? Someone to help her figure out what they needed to do. Someone like RJ.

She also knew she couldn't do it. This wasn't his problem. And if she told him, he'd make it his problem.

"So, what's the plan, Cook?"

Sugar was afraid she knew the plan, but she needed to ask anyway.

Cookie's expression crumbled. "I don't know. I'm scared and I don't know what to do. I know you will."

Yep, that's exactly what Sugar had suspected. She was the one who had to come up with the plan.

Story of my life.

She squashed a sigh in mid-formation, but obviously not fast enough.

"I'm sorry." Cookie shook her head. "I need help, and you know Mom and Dad won't be any. They'll tell me to figure it out and I just don't know what to do."

"Does anyone else know? Did you tell Candy?"

Candy and Cookie had always been attached at the hip as kids. They were only ten months apart in age and had done almost everything together growing up.

Candy didn't meet her gaze as she shook her head. "When I first found out, Candy was taking exams and I didn't want to mess that up for her."

Their sister had gotten a full ride to Penn State to study physics. Candy had always been book smart. No common sense at all, but then she'd had Sugar to handle all the stuff her brilliant brain just didn't have room for.

So Sugar understood. She did. She just... *Shit.* What the hell did they do next?

"Are you keeping it?"

"Him."

"You're having a boy?"

Cookie smiled genuinely for the first time, as if she'd finally remembered how.

"Yeah. I think we have enough girls in our family. Can't hurt to have a little more testosterone around."

"Do you want to keep him? There are options, you know."

Cookie's response was immediate. "He's mine and I want him. I just don't know what the hell to do."

Sugar wrapped her arms around Cookie and hugged her tight, her brain already kicking into gear.

"Then we'll figure it out. Together. Just like we always do."

"DISNEY WORLD. You're going to Florida for a week. In August. How did you get talked into that?"

"Because I'm a sucker, that's why." Dwayne Reid huffed out a breath as he deadlifted two-hundred pounds. "My kids know if they play the guilt card, they get to do whatever they want over the summer. Even if that means sweating my ass off in Florida for seven days while the kids have meltdowns and Angie threatens to ground them for the rest of their lives."

RJ shook his head, grinning even though his arms screamed from this third set of reps on the free weights. "Maybe you can get her to ground you and then you wouldn't have to go."

"Nah. She'll ground herself and send me alone with the three heathens."

"Your kids are great."

"Yeah, they are. Most of the time. That mean you wanna take 'em to Disney? Man, they would love that."

RJ laughed, as he was meant to do. Dwayne would never

give up time with his kids in the summer. Not when the season started in less than two months and there would be weeks he wouldn't see the kids at all except on a phone screen.

"Listen, man, when we get back, you have to come for dinner. Bring a date. Or, hell, just bring some woman you meet on the street. Bring someone because if you come alone, Angie's gonna be all over your ass to date her sister. And you do not want that crazy in your life."

RJ had to put the weights down before he dropped them. "Thanks for the heads-up. I think I may have the date covered."

Grabbing his towel from the nearby weight bench, he sat down and waited while Dwayne finished his reps. They'd been working out for the past hour late Sunday morning at the team training facility, and RJ still hadn't gotten around to the discussion he wanted to have.

Dwayne was the oldest member of the Colonials, and their friendship went back years. He wanted to talk to Dwayne about Rickie. He was still leaning toward no, but... Hell, he didn't know what he was going to say. He hoped Dwayne could help him make up his mind.

Dropping the weight bar on the floor, Dwayne grabbed his towel and water bottle and sat on the weight bench opposite RJ. They had the place pretty much to themselves, which was why they had a standing appointment Sunday mornings in the summer. Gave them time to connect. Talk.

But RJ still hadn't figured out how to broach the subject of Rickie.

"So, what's on your mind?" Dwayne asked. "You're been chewing on something since we got here. And since Angie and her sister took the kids down the shore, I've got the afternoon free. Spit it out."

"Dad asked me to take in Rickie Prescott. For the week of rookie camp."

Dwayne looked unimpressed and not at all surprised as he shrugged.

"Okay."

"Wait." RJ frowned, shaking his head. "Did you know?"

"Nah. But it makes sense. The kid's got a huge hero crush on you. Any time I've seen him interviewed, he mentions you. I get that you might not want the responsibility of an eighteen-year-old. If that's the problem, just say no."

"That's not it. It's just...I don't know. My dad said think about it. So I've been thinking."

Well, kind of. He'd been thinking mostly about Sugar.

He'd texted her this morning, asking about work. She'd replied:

`Hi. Busy. Another 12 hours today.`

He should've left well enough alone then, but he couldn't. Not with Sugar. So he'd asked if everything was okay. Because that short burst of words didn't sound like her.

"You have something else that's weighing on your mind?"

Dwayne's question came with a raised eyebrow.

Was he really that transparent?

"Maybe."

"And is this something else female perhaps? Because, you know, it's not like you're supposed to put your life on hold for a week just for a kid. He's eighteen, not ten. You don't have to supervise every minute of his day. Unless you're having wild orgies that you haven't invited me to, I think you're gonna be okay. But if it's gonna make you miserable—"

"No, it's not that. It's... There might be a woman."

Now, he had Dwayne's full attention, his brows perfect arches over his eyes.

"Damn, man. I would've taken bets that a woman wouldn't be in the picture. Glad to hear there is. Who is she?"

RJ shook his head. "No one you know. And we've literally had two—uh…"

Hmm. Couldn't really call them dates when basically all they did was have sex.

Dwayne's laugh filled the room, ringing off the walls. "I think I know what you're trying to say. Don't hurt yourself trying to figure out what to call it. So who is she?"

"Someone I've known for the past year. Our relationship took an unexpected turn recently."

"Unexpected, huh? That's a new word for getting laid."

RJ grimaced. "It's not just sex. I like her."

"Yeah, it's usually better when you like the person you're sleeping with."

"Are you just gonna keep chirping me or are you gonna shut up and listen?"

Dwayne's grin made RJ roll his eyes. "Hey, man, I'm listening. But you're not saying a whole lot that makes sense."

Shit. "I know. That's because I don't know what the hell's going on."

"Where'd you meet her?"

"At the diner near my place. She's a waitress."

"And?"

"And what? We've gotten together two nights so far."

"So it's just sex."

"It doesn't feel like just sex. At least, not to me."

"You want more?"

"I… Yeah. I guess. I do. I'm just not sure what she wants."

"Shit, it's been two nights and you wanna pick out china patterns?"

"When you say it like that, I guess I am jumping the gun."

"Only if you don't know if you want to see her again. If you know there's something there, then full speed ahead. You're not a kid anymore, you know."

"She's younger."

Dwayne's brows rose and the look he gave RJ made him shake his head.

"Not that young. She's twenty-three."

"Still don't see a problem."

"Maybe she's not looking for anything serious. And I've got a lot of shit going on in my life."

"No, you don't." Dwayne's expression was dead serious. "You left that shit behind in California. You were *cleared* of that shit. And maybe you just need to ask her what she wants. Now, what other excuses you got?"

"You're a pain in my ass."

Dwayne's laughter filled the room. "Just keeping you honest. Look, I'm not saying you shouldn't be pissed as hell about what happened in L.A. None of it was your fault. So why the hell are you still beating yourself up about it? You act like you don't deserve to be happy and that's fucked up."

Was that how he felt? That he didn't deserve to be happy?

"You think I should say no to having Rickie?"

"Hell no. I think you go after the girl *and* take the kid. You need to get back to normal. This kind of shit's totally normal for you. What's her name?"

"Sugar."

For the first time, Dwayne looked surprised. "Seriously? Her name's Sugar?"

"Yeah. And it fits her."

"Oh man, you look like you're already gone over this girl. It's nice to see. We've been worried about you."

"What? 'We' who?"

"Your friends. Your teammates. A few of us have talked about it. We just don't know how to help. Although Lad did suggest we get you laid. Guess the bastard had the right idea."

Grinning, Dwayne stood and offered his hand to pull RJ to his feet. RJ took it and let himself be helped.

"That little punk doesn't have a clue what he's talking about when it comes to women."

"That little punk outweighs you by twenty pounds. You're just pissed he was right. When're you gonna see her again?"

"Thursday. I'm taking her to Shane's. She works most nights."

"You wanna see her before then, take her to lunch."

"What are you? A matchmaker?"

Dwayne got a good laugh at that. "Maybe I should be. Sounds like you need some help in the dating department."

"And you're gonna help me? Dude, you've been married for more than a decade. What do you know about dating anymore?"

"Why do you think my wife still loves me? Let me give you a few pointers."

* * *

HOPE YOU HAVE a good night at work. Looking forward to seeing you Thursday.

Sugar stared at the text from RJ on her break Tuesday night, trying not to overheat. Or sigh like a lovesick idiot.

She was having a sucktastic night, and she didn't want to be here. She'd picked up an extra shift at Nero's this week, thinking it couldn't be as bad as the weekend. But even on a good night, she didn't want to be here. She'd been overlooking the sleaze factor for so long she'd thought she could handle anything, but tonight...

"Hey, Shug." Creeper Chris the manager stuck his head through the break-room door and yelled over the thumping music from the dance floor. "I need you to wait on Suite Two.

Dezzy's running behind and these guys are big tippers. Trust me, you'll thank me."

Before she had a chance to respond, the short, round slug who ran this club disappeared back into the bar, leaving Sugar staring at the door like she could set it on fire with her mind.

Her feet hurt in the three-inch heels the club required of all their female servers. Her black skirt was wet from where she'd had to blot out a drink some asshole had spilled on her, and she'd already changed her sheer black top for an identical one after a girl had stumbled off the dance floor and knocked Sugar into another waitress whose tray had launched a used appetizer plate directly at her boobs.

And now...Suite Two.

She wanted to text RJ: *Having a shitty night. My sister's knocked up. About to be felt up by drunk assholes who think money makes it ok. And I miss you.*

Which was stupid, because she'd seen him last night at the diner. He'd been by for dinner, and they'd talked and flirted, and life had seemed normal for a couple of hours. Then he left, and she closed the diner at midnight and went back to her apartment to sleep on the couch because her pregnant sister was in her bed.

And there was no way in hell she could text him how much she loathed working here. He already didn't like that she worked here. Neither did she, but up until a few seconds ago, she'd been ready to suck it up and head back to the floor, thinking of all the money she'd make tonight. Money she was going to need because her sister was about to have a baby and had come to Sugar for help because Cookie knew Sugar wouldn't let her swing out there on her own.

Now...

Shit. Just *shit.*

"You could just walk out, you know."

Sugar sucked in a deep breath and shook her head at Kyann, who'd been sucking down antacid when Chris had stuck his head in.

"And forfeit the money I earned this weekend? No way."

Kyann shrugged, D-cups jiggling under her top. "I get it but, hon, you look miserable tonight. Something else going on?"

Since she and Kyann were more coworkers than friends, Sugar shook her head and forced a smile. "Just the general shittiness of this place. Guess I better get out there before Creeper throws a fit."

Kyann chuckled at the waitstaff's nickname for the manager. "I hear you. I swear if one more asshole 'accidentally' touches my ass tonight, there will be crushed balls."

Tossing a grin of commiseration over her shoulder on the way out the door, Sugar headed for the second floor, trying to breathe through the tightness in her chest and unkink the knot in her stomach.

It didn't work. In fact, it only got worse the closer she got to her destination. Fuck it. Anyone touched her, she'd break their nose and worry about the consequences later. Turning the handle, she loosened her jaw and put on what she hoped was a pleasant expression. At least, she hoped it didn't look like she wanted to strangle someone with her bare hands. Or puke on them.

The noise hit her first.

Lots of men shouting and laughing over each other. Not angry, just loud. Everything about it made her cringe. They were celebrating some deal they'd closed. Real estate. Stocks. She didn't have a clue and didn't care.

She started making her way around the room, taking orders from men who either looked right though her or looked down at her tits and not at her face. A few of them actually thanked her before dismissing her. More than a few others looked her up and down like she was a cow they were going to buy. And then there was Tom.

"Hey there. I'm Tom. You're a beautiful woman. When you bring my drink back, bring one for you, too. I know the owner. I'll tell him not to fire you for drinking on the job. Trust me, he'll want you to make me happy."

Tom was fifty-something, bald and paunchy, and thought he had the right to put his arm around her.

Sugar sidestepped him the first time. "We're busy." She didn't even bother to cover the sneer in her tone. "What can I get you to drink?"

"Ah, babe, you're breaking my heart. Come on. What's one drink?"

Enough to make her want to puke down the front of this guy's thousand-dollar suit.

"Sorry." *Not on her life.* "What'll it be."

She could see the answer in his eyes. He wanted her to give him what he'd asked for. Out loud, he ordered a bottle of top-shelf bourbon. Sugar escaped before he could say or do anything else and make her haul off and hit him. Then she really wouldn't be getting paid.

It didn't take as long as she'd hoped to get the order filled at the upstairs bar. Apparently, whoever had rented Suite Two for the night had paid a lot of money to keep the liquor flowing. Grabbing the tray, she headed back to the suite. This time, she didn't bother putting on a smile. She just wanted to get in and get out as fast as possible, without breaking the tray over anyone's head. She'd distributed the drinks and was about to make a clean getaway when Tom decided he wasn't finished with her.

"Hey, why are you running away so fast? Have a drink." He put his hand on her arm. "You don't need to be such a bitch."

She tugged, trying to get her arm away from the asshole who

had dared to grab her, but he held on. She had a brief moment of panic as his hand tightened before she ripped her arm away.

Tom looked stunned for a second, but she could see what he was planning. Taking a step back, Sugar stared up at the man whose face was getting redder by the second.

"Touch me again and I will call the police."

Then she turned and stalked toward the door, grabbing the tray as she went. She was about to step through it when she heard a commotion behind her. In the hall, she turned back to see a few of the men holding good old Tom by the shoulders and another man with a grim look on his face following her.

She was about to make a run for the bar at the end of the hall when the guy held up his hands. Probably only a few years older than her, he looked upset and embarrassed.

"We're celebrating the close of a big deal and he's drunk. He won't be a problem again." Then he reached into his pocket and handed her a wad of cash. "A little something to say thank you."

She wanted to throw that money in his face. She also knew she couldn't afford to. So she took it.

Hazard pay.

Then she turned and walked back to the break room. Where she told Chris what had happened. To his credit, he got pissed and sent one of the security guys up to talk with the group. When he turned back to her, he started shaking his head, as if he could clearly read her intention on her face.

"Sugar, don't—"

"That guy could've broken my arm before anyone got to him. This job isn't worth—"

"Look, I've dealt with the guy. He won't be back. Just...take the rest of the night off. Don't make a decision you're going to regret later. Give it a day."

He walked away before she could respond. Standing in the

center of the now-empty room, she took a couple of deep breaths before she pulled out her phone.

It was one-fifty-five a.m. RJ had probably been asleep for hours already. He had the kids' camp starting tomorrow. He'd texted her last around eleven p.m., telling her to have a good night.

She wanted to talk to him so badly, she could barely breathe.

`Shitty from start to finish. Leaving ea`

"Hey, Sugar," another of the girls stuck her head in the break room. "I could use some help—what's wrong?"

"*Shit*."

Sugar looked down at her phone. She'd accidentally sent her unfinished email to RJ. She wanted to delete it immediately, but her fingers had started to shake, and she just wanted to get the hell out of here now.

"I'm leaving. Sorry, Dita. I'm out."

She put on a fresh shirt, grabbed her sneakers, and changed out her heels.

"Whoa, Shug. You sure you're okay? Want me to call you a ride?"

"No. I should make the next bus. I just...need to get out of here tonight. And if you have to put up with Suite Two, make sure you stay away from the asshole named Tom."

"Thanks for the heads-up."

Sugar bounced back onto her feet, ready to head for the door when her phone vibrated.

`Bad night? You ok?`

RJ was still awake. The need to see him was like a physical ache in her gut. She sucked in a sharp breath and responded before she took a second to think through a response.

`Yes.`

`Wanna stop by?`

God, yes. She absolutely wanted to stop by. She could text her sister and tell her she'd see her in the morning. Cookie was probably already asleep, and if she needed Sugar, she could call. It wasn't like she was going to give birth tonight.

`Don't you have to be up early tomorrow?`

`I can survive on a couple hours sleep. Rather spend the time with you.`

She blinked, stupid tears at the corners of her eyes.

`OK. Will see you in a few.`

`Need a lift?`

She didn't want to drag him out this late at night. But—

"Sugar." Chris stuck his head through the door. "I got you a ride. Car's here."

Holy shit. Chris must really feel guilty. More like he didn't want to lose another waitress during their busiest season or have her bring the cops in.

"Okay. Be right there."

`No. Thanx. Be there in a few.`

`Look forward to it.`

The driver waiting for her was a woman, which Sugar appreciated more than she could say. She'd had enough of men for the night. Except for one man.

You know it's not going to last, right? You're just a diversion. The rebound.

She realized she was gritting her teeth and made a conscious effort to loosen her jaw. She hated that voice in her head, but it had been whispering in her ear all night and she hadn't been able to shut it up.

"You look exhausted, sweetie. Hope you're heading home."

Sugar smiled at the older woman looking at her in the rearview mirror, shaking her head.

"Actually, I'm heading to my...um, friend's house."

Friend. Is that what she should call RJ? He wasn't exactly

her boyfriend, but she did consider him a friend. She had for the past several months. And now they were... What?

The driver grinned at her before pulling the car away from the curb.

"From the smile on your face, I'm thinking this *friend* is more than that. Maybe one with benefits."

Sugar smiled but honestly didn't know how to respond. Which just made the little voice in her head louder.

You're just a piece on the side, a diversion until he finds another woman who'll fit into his life. Not some uneducated waitress with a pregnant sister to support.

After giving the driver the address of RJ's apartment building, Sugar settled into the backseat, determined to ignore that voice. But the closer she got to his apartment, the more insistent it became.

Why haven't you told him about Cookie? Because you think he'll drop you so fast it'll make your head spin? Hell, he may feel sorry for you because he's such a nice guy but you're just not right for him, are you?

Jesus, how did she make this stop?

It didn't take long to get to RJ's at this time of night, and by the time she thanked the driver and slid out of the car, she had to take a couple of deep breaths to calm down.

You're fine. Everything's going to be fine. It's not like you're in love with the guy. It's just sex. Right?

Just thinking that one four-letter word made her brain stutter and pop like a fuse short-circuiting.

Stop. Just...stop.

Sucking in a breath, she forced her brain to shut off and headed for the lobby.

A different security guard, a little older and grayer, stood behind the desk and, once again, she got the up-and-down assessment. Her blood began a slow boil. She was in no mood to deal with another asshole male.

"I'm here to see RJ Mitchell."

"Name?"

"Sugar Donahue."

His brows rose. "Your parents actually named you Sugar?"

She stopped a sigh in mid-formation. "Yeah, they actually did."

"Huh. Thought RJ was yanking my chain. Go on up. Know where you're going?"

"I do."

"Then have a good night, Miss Donahue."

She mustered a smile for the guy who was only doing his job. "You too."

Okay, maybe all men weren't jerks.

Just most of them

Ugh. Make it stop! She wanted to throw a full-fledged tantrum, which would only prove she wasn't mature enough for RJ.

And that was a load of bullshit, because for as long as she could remember, she'd been the most mature person in her family, and she was including her parents in that count. There was a reason Cookie had come to her instead of to their parents. There was a reason her youngest sister had sobbed like someone had died the day Sugar had left.

Damn it, when did she get to be the one who needed to be taken care of?

Now you're just feeling sorry for yourself. When you should be focusing on the fact that you're about to see RJ and you don't want to be a bitch.

Because, honestly, she wasn't sure how often she'd get to see him in the future. They'd just found each other and now there were all these roadblock—

God, just stop.

The elevator stopped, and she practically ran down the hall to his door. Which opened before she had a chance to knock.

"Hey—"

She stood on her toes and wrapped her arms around his shoulders, cutting off whatever he'd been about to say by sealing her lips over his. She kissed him like she needed him to breathe. And tonight, maybe she did. Maybe she needed him to wipe her brain clean and replace it with memories of him. The way he kissed her. The way he touched her, the way he smelled, and the feel of his hands gripping her hips and pulled her against his hard, ready body.

If she'd surprised him, he recovered in a split second. He wrapped one arm around her waist and lifted her off the ground while he shut the door behind them. As he started to walk, she lifted her legs to wrap them around his waist. Both hands landed on her ass, holding her in place and petting her, like he couldn't wait to touch her.

She knew he was moving toward the bedroom, and her already overexcited emotions heightened every sensation. By the time he sat on the bed and lowered them down to the mattress, with her knees on either side of his thighs and her body plastered flat against his, she thought she might crawl out of her skin.

Only the crush of his mouth against hers and his hands roaming her body shut down all the questions pounding away at her brain.

They made out like horny teenagers for long minutes, all lips and tongues tangled and hands stroking and petting. But unlike a teenager, RJ knew exactly what to do with his hands. He stroked and kneaded and petted her with the sole purpose of making her crazy for him.

His fingers knew exactly where to touch her to make her

gasp into his mouth as she grinded her hips into his. His erection was a stiff rod beneath his gym shorts and his t-shirt clung to his chest like a lover. For tonight, that chest was hers and she wanted it exposed.

Sitting up, she looked into his eyes, burning hot with desire for her. Making sure he was watching, she shoved her hands under his shirt, wanting to lick her lips at the heat of his skin against her palms.

"Take this off. Please."

He grinned at her demand, the purely sexual curve of his mouth making hers water. Without a word, he crunched forward, grabbed the back of his shirt with one hand, and pulled it over his head. She swallowed hard at the sight of his abs doing all that work before she put her hands on his shoulders and followed him back down to the mattress.

Her mouth went to his throat, kissing a trail down to his chest, as his hand tangled in her hair. She'd forgotten she'd pulled it back in a ponytail until he tugged out the band and her hair spilled around her face.

In the next second, he gathered it in one hand and held it at her nape. The slight tug as she kissed her way down his chest sent tingles through her body, caused her core to clench and ache. She stopped to suck and nip at his nipples before continuing her journey down his body to her destination.

His stomach contracted under her lips as she stopped just below his belly button. Looking back up at him, she saw he'd lost the grin. This look blistered her with its intensity as she yanked down his shorts and exposed his cock.

"Thanks for skipping the underwear."

"You're—*fuck*."

She sucked the tip of his cock into her mouth, swirled her tongue around the tip then sank down the shaft as far as she could go. She felt every muscle in RJ's body go taut as his cock throbbed in her mouth.

"Holy shit, Sugar."

His hand tightened in her hair until she had to strain to take him in all the way. Every time she did, her pussy ached a little more, goaded on by the rough sounds he made. She loved those sounds, loved the way her scalp burned and nipples throbbed.

When she knew he was close, she pulled back to the tip and sucked hard, trying to push him over the edge. But he stubbornly refused to go.

"Sugar. Take this. Then fuck me."

He pulled her hair with enough force to make her look up. He held a condom in his hand. Time to make a decision.

She wanted him inside her when he came. She wanted to ride him until he came.

Scrambling off the bed, she shoved down her shorts and panties and pulled her tank top over her head. She hadn't been wearing a bra, and when his gaze dropped, her nipples peaked as if he'd touched her.

She reached for the condom, but he was already rolling it down his erection. Scrambling back onto the bed on her knees, she sank onto his cock in one smooth move that made them both suck in air.

"Christ, Sugar. You're so tight."

With her hands planted on his chest, she started to ride him, watching his face as she did. She was making him feel like this, making him gasp out her name and grip her hips so tight it hurt.

Moaning, she rode him hard, chasing an orgasm she felt building deep inside. God, she wanted him so desperately, her heart hurt. Her entire body strained toward that feeling she knew he could give her. Opening her eyes, which she hadn't realized she'd closed, she looked down at RJ.

He was watching her, so much burning passion on his face

she felt her pussy clench in response. She sank down, rolling her hips to rub her clit against the base of his cock. It was exactly what she needed.

She came around him, gripping him tight as she sank down to his chest, tucking her head under his chin. He held still for a few precious seconds, his breath rough in her ear.

Then he wrapped his arms around her. Tight. So tight. And he flipped them without dislodging from her still-spasming pussy.

"Wrap your legs around my waist and hold tight."

She barely heard his words, but she understood what he wanted. The coiled tension in his body transmitted to her and she lifted her heavy legs to grip his hips. The motion sent another ripple of ecstasy through her. Her eyes fluttered closed as her arms wrapped around his ribs to clutch at his back.

Planting his elbows above her shoulders, he thrust, seating himself even deeper than she thought he could possibly go. Then he retreated, the drag of his cock on her overly sensitive sheath sweet torture.

His first thrusts were slow, smooth. Spreading her wide and staking his claim. His lips spread a line of fire from just behind her ear to the point of her chin, before taking her mouth in a kiss that stole her breath.

Then he started to move in earnest.

His hips snapped against hers, setting a punishing pace that pushed her body into a physical state between pleasure and almost-pain and her mind into a trance-like state. She held on tight, sucking on his tongue as he ravaged her mouth and pussy.

For several long seconds, they were locked in a sensual dance. And when he finally broke away, she sucked in a deep breath, raking her nails down his back and making him groan.

"God, Sugar. You feel so fucking good."

"Don't stop. Don't stop."

"Never. *Fuck.*"

His hips snapped again and again, his breath rough against her cheek. She could barely move, but she needed...something. Tilting her hips up a fraction was all it took.

The angle of penetration changed, and RJ froze for a split second before he buried his face in her neck and thrust deep one more time as he came.

"BAD NIGHT, HUH?"

Sugar sighed as she snuggled closer to RJ. They were still trying to catch their breath, even after RJ had been to the bathroom and returned to tuck Sugar into his bed. He'd crawled in next to her, drew her into his side, and wove his fingers into her hair as she rested her head on his chest.

She wanted to stay right here for as long as he'd let her.

"Yes. Just a couple of assholes who made the night miserable."

"That happen a lot at Nero's?"

"Yeah. But it's good money."

And right now, she needed as much as she could get her hands on. Cookie's pregnancy changed everything.

He didn't respond right away, which was probably a good thing. They'd already had this discussion. She knew he didn't like that she worked there, but she needed the money. No contest.

"I'm not sure what the money's like, but the owners of the ice complex where we hold camp are looking for someone to run their concessions. If it's something you think you'd be interested in, I could say something to the manager. It's full-time with benefits. Can't guarantee the salary would be amazing but can't hurt to ask."

Full-time. An actual, reliable schedule. Benefits. RJ's involvement would guarantee her an interview, something she'd probably never get on her own. And with her experience in a kitchen and recommendations from Georgie and Janine, she might actually have a shot. With a steady schedule, she could still waitress.

"That would be great. If you think it's something I'm qualified for."

"I'll say something to Dominique tomorrow. She's been looking for someone for a couple months, so I'm thinking the pay might not be great. Just a heads-up. And you have to be able to handle chaos."

"Chaos I can handle. Wandering hands, not so much."

RJ stilled, and she wanted to take back the words immediately. Damn it, she didn't want to make this into an issue. Then again, maybe they should just rip off the bandage and get it over with.

"What exactly happened tonight?"

"Just some drunk guy who wanted me to have a drink with him. I handled it. I *can* handle myself."

He was quiet for a few seconds. "I know. I'm not saying you can't. I'm just saying maybe that's not the safest environment for you."

She shrugged, like he was overstating the issues. "The money's too good to pass up."

Another short pause. "I've seen how men act when they're there. They're assholes. You shouldn't have to work with them."

"Actually, no woman should have to work there. But we still like to eat." She heard the edge in her voice and took it down a notch. "Besides, I never work there more than two days a week. Some nights it just gets to me. This was just one of those nights."

"So get out."

Like it'd be easy to just find another job that paid what Nero's did. "All jobs have things you don't like about them."

"Find something else."

Her teeth clenched. "It's not that easy."

"I'll talk to the complex manager."

"I don't need you to find me a job. I don't even know if I'm qualified."

"Everybody needs help. Sometimes, you just need to take it."

"And sometimes you can't just snap your fingers and make things happen. Life just doesn't work that way. At least not for people like me. And if you think that, then you don't really know me."

EIGHT

RJ's brain spun as Sugar sighed.

What the hell had he said?

They'd just had the most amazing sex he'd ever experienced in his life then the conversation had taken a left turn, and he wasn't sure how to get them back on track. Because anything he said now had the potential to be a landmine. But he didn't understand why she wouldn't want his help.

He understood standing on your own two feet. Hell, he'd had to work harder at everything to prove he deserved his career and wasn't just coasting on his dad's reputation. But sometimes, you needed a hand and shouldn't be ashamed to accept it.

Hell, Marisol would've been perfectly happy to let him use his influence to get her whatever she'd wanted.

Maybe that should've been a clue that the only reason she was with you was to snag a professional athlete husband and let him take care of her for the rest of her life.

He didn't want to be someone's meal ticket. He wanted a partner. He liked that Sugar was independent. He admired the hell out of her. And he thought she was sexy as fuck.

Maybe you should tell her that.

"Then tell me about you. I want to know everything."

The words came out before he thought them through, but they were true.

He wanted her to tell him everything about her life. They were sharing a bed after having awesome sex, and he realized he wanted more. Of her. Of her life. Not just the few hours a day they spent in bed.

And she was still silent. He could practically hear her thinking, though, until finally, she said, "Does that go both ways?"

A split-second decision. "What do you want to know?"

Her breath feathered across his chest as she lifted her head then propped her chin on his chest so she could look at him.

"What's your favorite color?"

"Blue."

"Your favorite TV show?"

"*Law & Order.*"

Her nose crinkled in confusion. "Seriously?"

"Yeah. No matter what part of the show I tune into, I know where I am because I've seen it already and some channel is always running one of them."

Her laughter sank into his gut like a knife, burrowing down until he didn't think it'd ever be dislodged.

"Okay, I'll give you that one. But that has to be the most 'guy' answer ever."

"Well, I'm a guy so..."

"Yes, you are."

Before he got sidetracked by the way her smile heated his blood, he said, "My turn. Do you have any nights off next weekend so we can go on an actual date?"

Something flickered through her expression, something that made his breath catch.

"I would love that, yeah." Her smile turned his apprehension into full-blown heat. "I think Wednesday night might work, if you don't mind going late?"

He wanted to say yes, but... "I've got to make an appearance at a teammate's party."

"Oh. That's no pro—"

"Come with me."

She blinked and surprise flashed across her face, followed by an emotion that looked like hope.

"Sure. I mean, if you don't mind?"

"Why would I mind?"

"Well, because they're your friends and I wouldn't want to get in the way?"

The lilt at the end of her sentence made his grin widen.

"You wouldn't be in the way. I wouldn't have asked if I didn't want you with me."

It took a few seconds but finally, her smile reappeared. "Okay. Sure."

"Good. And we're still on for tomorrow, right?" When she nodded, he said, "Good. Now, what are you doing the rest of the week after work?"

Her gaze skipped away and back again. "I'm not sure." She grinned, but he could tell it wasn't as genuine as her last. "There're things I have to get done."

He wanted to press, but he didn't want to push her. Well, yeah, he wanted to push her, but he didn't want to push her away.

"No problem. I'm flexible."

Her expression eased and a tease lit in her eyes. "Yes, you are."

"I don't think you're talking about my schedule right now."

"You'd be right."

Slipping his hands beneath her arms, he pulled her up his body until he could reach her lips.

With his lips against hers, he said, "Let me show you just how flexible I can be."

———

"I SWEAR this kid is trying to kill me. I have to pee every five minutes. I can't sleep more than five minutes before he kicks me in the kidneys. My back aches. My boobs hurt. And where were you last night?"

Sugar had definitely not had enough sleep for this conversation. But with her sister sitting across from her at the table, staring at her with her brows raised Wednesday at six a.m., waiting for an answer, she didn't have the brain power to think up a lie.

"With a friend."

"And were you having sex with this friend? Because I hope you used a condom. It'd be pretty bad if we both got knocked up."

Sugar sighed, which turned into a yawn. She'd thought she could get home and get a few more hours of sleep before she had to get to work. But Cookie had been sitting on the couch, eating ice cream at eight in the morning, watching some serial killer documentary that would've given Sugar nightmares.

"At least tell me you had fun."

"I really don't want to talk about it now. I'm tired and I need to go to work in, like, two hours."

"But you worked last night?"

"And I have to work again today. The bills don't pay themselves."

She hadn't meant that to sound as harsh as it had, and when she looked up with an apology on the tip of her tongue, she saw

Cookie wince and turn her head, her hands coming to rest on her belly.

"Damn it, I didn't mean that like it sounded. I'm sorry. I'm tired. And I know that's no excuse but—"

"Stop." Cookie shrugged. "It's okay. I shouldn't have pushed. I really am grateful you took me in. I know this isn't what you expected to be doing with your life. And I swear, I won't be here forever. I just needed a place—"

"Cook, shut up." Sugar grabbed her sister's hand across the table. "I'm cranky and bitchy and tired. And how can I keep an eye on you if you were anywhere else?"

"I just..." Her sister grimaced apologetically. "I want this baby so much. I know you probably think that's stupid, but—"

"No. I don't think that at all. Of course, you want your baby. We'll figure it out. I promise."

Cookie smiled, relief in every sweet curve of her face. "I know. But you still didn't tell me who you were with last night."

Shaking her head, she sighed and slumped back into her chair. "He's just a guy I know."

"Just a guy? If you're having sex with him, he's not just some guy. You're not into casual. You never have been."

"We haven't even been on a date. Between my schedule and his, it's just...complicated."

"But you *have* been sleeping with him. So, who is he? Is he nice? Do you like him?"

"Of course, I like him. I wouldn't be sleeping with him if I didn't."

Cookie rolled her eyes. "I mean, do you *really* like him? How long have you known him?"

Uneasy now, she shrugged. "For about a year."

"You've been sleeping with the guy for a year but haven't had a date yet?"

The shock in Cookie's tone made Sugar wince. "No, that's

not what I meant. We met a year ago. He walked into the diner, and I felt like I'd been punched in the gut. And then he smiled at me, and my brain short-circuited. I was barely able to talk to him without making an ass out of myself. I couldn't look at him without wanting to throw myself at him. And I don't think he even noticed me until a few weeks later. I mean, he was always nice to me, never treated me like I was beneath him, you know. He's just...a really nice guy."

"Damn, Shug, he sounds almost too good to be true." Cookie gave a disgusted little huff. "I met my baby daddy at a bar and the first thing I noticed was his ass. Probably should've been my first clue that it wasn't going to work."

Sugar laughed, which was exactly what Cookie had intended.

"Is he totally out of the picture?"

Shrugging, Cookie's gaze slid away. "I assume he is. And even if he came back, I'm not sure I'd take him back. The way we left it was...not that friendly."

"Should I be worried about him showing up here?"

"No." Cookie shook her head emphatically. "He's not like that. Actually, I think I'm the one who fucked things up."

"Don't be too hard on yourself. It's a tough time for you. I mean, you're baking a little human inside you. You get a few passes for bad behavior."

"I don't want to fuck this up, Shug. And up until now, that's all I've done to everything."

Sugar didn't want to tell Cookie that wasn't true because, yeah, Cookie had always been in and out of trouble growing up. Nothing ever really bad. But she'd always pushed the boundaries. Their parents had let her run wild and it'd always been up to Sugar to rein her back in. And then Sugar had left.

Not your fault.

No, but here was Cookie, her long blonde hair in braids that made her look about fifteen and a huge belly that made it clear she had some pretty adult problems on her plate.

"Everybody makes mistakes. We'll figure it out together."

It just might mean Sugar had to give up the one thing she wanted for herself.

"I'M sorry I didn't say anything sooner. It's been so busy, and I just couldn't find the time, and I know I'm the only one on the lease but—"

"Now, that's nothing you need to worry about." Georgie sliced her hand through the air, as if cutting off the conversation. "She's your sister."

"But—"

"Does she need anything right now? Does she have an obstetrician? Janine knows a couple. She can get Cookie in to see one today or tomorrow if she needs to. What is she? Eight months? Is she taking her vitamins?"

As Georgie continued on with a litany of questions she hadn't even considered, Sugar blinked back tears. For the first time in forever, she felt like she had a support system, rather than being the support system.

And when Georgie paused to text Janine for phone numbers, Anika offered up boxes of baby clothing that were "just taking up space" in her storage area.

The diner hadn't opened yet Wednesday morning and only Crystal, who baked and helped cook weekday mornings, Georgie, Anika, and Sugar were in the place. Sugar had hoped to get Georgie alone before the morning rush started, but Georgie and Crystal had already been in full swing by the time Sugar had shown up. And because they'd been busy, Sugar had had to tell them while they worked. Anika had walked in midway through her explanation and then she'd had to circle back and fill her friend in on what'd she'd missed.

Sugar had been dreading this conversation. She'd wanted to have it yesterday but had never found the time to get Georgie alone. Sugar had literally walked into the kitchen, put her apron on, and shuttled food for ten hours.

She shouldn't have been worried. Georgie's response shouldn't be a surprise. Most people were kind, wanted to lend a hand. Sugar just wasn't used to taking the help. She was always the one being asked for help.

"You okay, Shug? You look a little overwhelmed. Crystal, give the girl one of those sticky buns. Those things have enough sugar to juice you for days."

"Thank you, Georgie."

As she took the cinnamon- and icing-laden roll from the bakery chef, Sugar hoped Georgie knew that gratitude wasn't just for the food.

"Not needed. Just eat your bun then open the door. Oh, and I need you to run the lunch food over to RJ's camp today. Our regular runner called in sick and Janine's having trouble with her foot so she can't drive."

Which was how she found herself, four hours later, shivering next to a huge sheet of ice, watching RJ skate backwards, followed by about twenty kids of various sizes, most of them screaming wildly. RJ's smile made her heart pound and her mouth water.

How could doing something as simple as skating make this man so damn sexy? And she wasn't the only person who noticed. She'd been standing there watching him for several minutes, the rolling cart she'd used to bring in lunch forgotten by her side, pretty much oblivious to everything that wasn't RJ.

The not-so-dead women sitting in the stands, stainless

thermal mugs clenched in their manicured hands, finally registered on Sugar when she heard one of them say his name.

"I would love to get that man in a bed. RJ goes to my gym
and, holy crap, he is built like a fucking Greek god. I can't
believe he's single."

"That won't last forever. Some skinny blonde puck bunny'll
tie him around her finger."

"He's such a nice guy. Have you talked to him? He just
seems like he's genuinely interested in whatever you're saying."

"If I ever got the guy alone, we wouldn't be talking."

Their conversation was barely loud enough for Sugar to
hear over the noise of the kids on the ice, but once she tuned
into them, their voices became clear. She assumed they were
there to watch their kids, though she couldn't blame them for
wanting to take a bite out of RJ. She certainly did.

And tomorrow, you'll get to.

She grinned, taking a few more steps to reach the glass. RJ
looked over at that moment and spotted her, the smile creasing
his lips making it hard for her to breathe.

"Who's he smiling at?"

"My god, could that man get any hotter? Seriously."

"Kinda young for him, isn't she?"

That last one threatened to suck a little of the joy out of her,
but she refrained from responding, even though she was pretty
sure they knew she'd been listening to them. And what did it
matter? She was the one who'd been in his bed Sunday night.
And hopefully would be again Wednesday night.

Holding up his forefinger in her direction with a question in
his eyes, she nodded, knowing he'd asked her to stay.

The lunch rush was probably in full swing by now, but
Georgie wouldn't have sent Sugar if she couldn't spare her. Not
that Sugar would stay that much longer, but she didn't want to

pass up the opportunity to talk to him, even if it was only for a few seconds.

Less than a minute later, the kids skated for the benches and the ice crew opened the large doors where she was standing. Moving to the side so they could do whatever they needed to do, she watched RJ bend down to pick up a little girl who'd fallen on her way. The little girl beamed up at him, talking nonstop as he got her caught up to the rest of the group.

"Okay, everyone, take off your skates and put on your sneakers and we'll get some lunch. Coach Jake's going to go with you, and I'll be there in a few minutes. Good job this morning. Get some food in you and we'll play a couple of games this afternoon."

The cheer that went up from the bench made Sugar laugh, her first natural laugh all day. RJ turned and skated back to her, taking off his helmet as he closed the distance between them.

But before he got to her, the moms called him by name, waving him over with smiles. She expected him to go. Instead, he nodded, waved, and skated over to Sugar.

"Hey, this is a nice surprise."

"The delivery guy had an emergency. You look like you're having a good time."

"I am. I forgot how much I love working with the little ones. They've got so much energy."

"I can't believe how coordinated they are. I'd be falling on my ass."

"Then we'll have to get you on skates, see how much you remember."

"I'd love to."

"They're having an open skate Sunday morning. If you don't work, we could come by then maybe go for brunch?"

She wanted to say yes, but it would mean leaving Cookie

most of Sunday because she was scheduled to work from three to eleven at Nero's. Cookie would roll her eyes and tell her to go.

When she didn't answer, RJ continued. "Unless you have something else to do?"

"I might. I have to work at three but... Can I get back to you? I just need to check something."

"Sure. No problem."

The words she needed to say burned the tip of her tongue. She wanted to tell him about her sister. Didn't know why she kept putting it off, but it wasn't something that came up in conversation easily. Especially not while they had an audience.

The women who'd wanted to talk to him had moved closer, clearly listening to their conversation while trying to make it look like they weren't.

She shouldn't care what they thought. Shouldn't care what anyone thought.

"Well, I should get back to work."

Nodding, he watched her take a few steps backward. "See you tomorrow, Sugar."

Turning, she hurried out before she could make a fool out of herself and steal the kiss she desperately wanted.

"YOU BRINGING SUGAR TOMORROW NIGHT? You know she's gonna be the center of attention, right? The women will be all over her. You sure you want to introduce her to everyone at once?"

"She'll know Tara. And the guys are all supposedly adults. Hopefully they'll be on their best behavior."

Brody's eyebrows rose. "Have you met our team? When are they ever on their best behavior? You're the only one with any manners."

RJ didn't respond because Brody wasn't entirely wrong. "At least Straka won't be there. He doesn't get back 'til August."

"Small favors. I like the guy, but..."

"He's an ass."

Couldn't argue with that either.

"You give Dad an answer yet?"

"No. And I know I need to. I just...haven't figured out what to tell him."

"Still leaning toward no?"

"Actually, I think I'm going to say yes."

Brody didn't bother to hide his surprise. "Good. Now you're more like yourself."

"I feel more like myself."

"Getting laid regularly will do that for a guy."

Brody grabbed the throw pillow he'd been resting his arm on and threw it at his brother, laughing when it caught Brody off-guard.

"Dude. You mess up Tara's decorating and she *will* kick your ass."

Brody and Tara had recently moved in together and Brody's once-barren apartment, decorated only with books and hockey-related apparatus, had transformed into an explosion of color and comfort. Throw pillows, soft rugs, and actual pictures on the walls.

And Brody was happier than RJ had ever seen him. All due to Tara.

"Tara likes me. And she'd totally understand if I had to mess up her decorating to kick your butt." His phone buzzed in his pocket and he checked the number. "*Shit.*"

"What's wrong?"

RJ turned his phone toward Brody so he could read the screen.

Brody's expression turned hard. "You need to block that number. And don't even think about answering that."

"I have no idea what she'd be calling about. I haven't talked to her in almost a year."

Marisol had made it clear the last time he'd talked to her that she wanted a clean break. No contact. No late-night hookups. No nothing. He'd agreed, even though he'd felt blindsided. Better to have no contact at all.

"Then you don't need to start now."

He was about to send the call to voice mail when it stopped ringing on its own. Shaking his head, he shoved the phone back into his pocket.

"Don't worry. I'm not interested in revisiting that relationship in any way."

"Glad to hear it. You seeing Sugar tonight?"

"No. She's working until eight and she has stuff to catch up on."

"Guess you can't just have sex all the time."

"You do have to eat sometimes."

"ARE you sure you're going to be okay? I don't want to leave you if you're not feeling well. What if you go into labor?"

Cookie rolled her eyes as she lay on the couch, looking so damn uncomfortable, Sugar cringed just watching her try to position herself.

"If I go into labor, I think you're gonna have enough time to get home before I deliver. Most first-time pregnancies take forever so even if you're an hour away, I think you'll get here in plenty of time."

Sugar worried her bottom lip, torn between leaving her sister alone for the night and going to a party with RJ. On one hand, she knew Cookie was right. She'd gone with her sister to her appointment yesterday morning and the baby doctor had said she probably had another two weeks to go. On the other, her sister was nineteen, pregnant, and alone.

Except for the diner full of people downstairs and Janine's and Georgie's numbers in her speed dial.

"Okay. But I want you to call me if anything changes. I mean anything."

"Yes, of course. If I actually pee longer five seconds, you'll know. Seriously, I'll be fine. I'm actually looking forward to having an entire night of alone time."

"I'm not sure I'll be out *all* night—"

"Oh please. Why wouldn't you spend the night at RJ's? When you have to spend the night at home alone, all you do is mope. Please. Just have a good time." Then she pointed at her belly and grinned. "But not too good."

Shaking her head, Sugar looked out the window at the street, trying to see RJ's car. She'd told him to text when he got there, and she'd come down to him. She wondered if he thought it was weird they never came to her place. Then again, they'd already tried her bed and found it didn't fit them.

"Should I be worried that I want to spend all my time with him?"

Sugar could see Cookie's reflection in the mirror, saw her sister's expression fall, and immediately wished she could take back the question.

"No, I think that's the way it's supposed to be, if you really like someone."

"I really like him."

"Yeah, I kinda figured that out. We were all really worried about you after Bobby's death. It's nice to see you starting to live again."

"I didn't stop living. I just..." She shrugged, not knowing

how to express how she'd felt. "I just couldn't find anything to be excited about. Does that make sense?"

"Of course, it does."

"RJ excites me." Her sister's grin kicked in again. "And I don't just mean that in a sexual way, so get your mind out of the gutter."

"Uh-huh."

"Although he's really freaking good in bed. I mean, like, oh my god, amazing."

Cookie's laughter rang through the small apartment just as she caught sight of RJ's car pulling up to the front of the building.

Pulling out her phone, she texted she'd be right down and turned to grab her purse.

"How do I look?"

"Like you plan to have sex all night. You look fine, Shug. You better get going or he's going to park and come looking for you. And I'm guessing you don't want to surprise him with the pregnant sister he doesn't know you have. And before you take that the wrong way, I'm not up for company, so get a move on."

Shit. Sugar looked down at herself, wondering if she should change for, like, the hundredth time. RJ had said they'd be outside, and it was summer in the city, so she'd worn a pretty, purple cami dress with a ruffled hem that hit midthigh, left most of her back bare and plainly showed she wasn't wearing a bra. And didn't need one.

Since she wouldn't know anyone other than Brody and Tara, she was a little afraid she was going to stand out.

Screw it.

Walking to the couch, she hugged Cookie before heading for the door.

"I'm not ashamed of you, you know that, right?"

"I know. Have fun tonight. Forget about the fact that I turned your life upside down for a few hours."

Like that was going to happen. "Love you. Call me if you need anything. An-y-thing."

Her sister saluted her as she headed out, knowing if she thought about this anymore, she wouldn't leave. But every step that took her closer to him, her heart felt a little lighter and the weight on her shoulders lifted.

And when she stepped out of her building, not even the soupy humidity of Philadelphia in August could drag down her spirits. The platform sandals made her feel even more feminine than the dress and when she stepped up to RJ, waiting for her by passenger door, she could almost kiss his chin if he tilted his head down and she tilted her head back. Almost.

"You look beautiful."

She'd never had anyone say that to her.

Stopping in her tracks, Sugar stared up at RJ, momentarily speechless. What was she supposed to say to that? All she could think of was, "Thank you," but that didn't seem enough. Not with the way those words in his voice made her feel.

But she said them anyway then tried not to let it show that she actually felt tears welling in her eyes. Everything she'd been keeping bottled inside wanted to spill out, but he'd probably think she was crazy. So she forced herself to smile, which wasn't that hard when she took a good look at him. Wearing a pair of khaki shorts and a dark blue t-shirt that stretched across his chest and made her want to pet him, he looked like every single one of her teenage fantasies come to life.

She'd never fallen for the bad boys. She'd been smart enough to know those boys only led to heartache. Of course, her first love had broken her heart in so many other ways. But RJ was the whole package. Sweet, smart, kind, considerate. A decent guy.

And while some girls might find that boring, she'd just smile and think about all the ways he was *not* boring in bed.

"I totally want to know what that smile is for but before we both melt, why don't we get in the car in the air conditioning? Then you can tell me what you're thinking."

Opening the door for her, he helped her into the leather passenger seat of his Grand Cherokee before shutting her door and getting into the driver's side. He stuck the key in the ignition but didn't start it right away.

Instead, he turned to look at her as she sat there and ate him up with her eyes.

"How was your day off?"

Perfect opening to tell him about Cookie. Except the words got stuck in her throat. "Busy, catching up on stuff around the house. Laundry. Cleaning." *Obstetrician visit.* "How was camp?"

His smile stole the air from her lungs. "Great. I love working with the little guys. So much fun. And you remember Danny, right? From the diner?"

When she nodded, his smile got even bigger.

"He's got a boatload of natural talent. I mean, the kid's only six but he can skate like he was born on ice and he can handle a stick while he skates, which is amazing at his age. I need to talk to his mom about getting him into a league this winter. Gotta figure out a way to funnel the money so his parents don't feel like it's charity, but it would be a damn shame if that kid didn't play."

Then he leaned across the middle console, put his hand on her chin, and kissed her with enough heat to make her thighs clench.

"I wanted to do that all day." Then he grinned. "But we better get going or we'll get arrested for public indecency. Have I told you how great you look?"

Then he turned the key, started the car, and pulled away from the curb. Even with the air blowing full blast, she felt like she was on fire from her core out.

"I want to apologize in advance for some of the guys," he said as he navigated through the city toward West Philadelphia. "Some of them aren't as civilized as they pretend to be."

"Will the whole team be there?"

"No. Some of the guys are still on vacation or visiting family. There'll probably be about thirty people, including the WAGs."

"Wags?"

"Wives and girlfriends."

Did she fit into that designation? The girlfriend designation?

"A lot of the guys who'll be here tonight played together in Reading, so they've known each for years. Come to think of it, I'll probably be the oldest guy there."

"Does that bug you?"

"That I'm older than most of them? Nah. I'm pretty comfortable with where I am in my life right now."

"At the top of your game?"

He flashed her a smile. "Been checking out the ESPN blog?"

Why did such a little thing like his smile make her forget her damn name? "Maybe I saw something scroll through my feed the other day and maybe I decided to read it."

"Well, don't believe everything you read. I've got to work twice as hard to stay where I am. Some days it's tough to find the motivation, but I'm doing what I love and not everyone can say that about their job."

"True. I mean, it's not like I grew up wanting to be a waitress, but I do like to eat, so there's that."

"Damn, forgot to tell you. I talked to Dominique at the rink. She said you should give her a call tomorrow about that job."

"Really?" Shock made her brain skip a few beats. "I wasn't sure... I mean... Thank you."

"For what?" His bemused smile made her breath catch in her throat. "I didn't demand they hire you. I just told Dominique you'd be a good fit and she should talk to you. No big deal."

But it was. Or it could be. Especially when the baby came, and she needed to know she'd have a regular paycheck.

"I wouldn't even have known about the job if you hadn't told me, so I still get to thank you. And I..."

She needed to tell him about Cookie. She wanted to tell him, but there was that little part of her brain that kept whispering, *Don't do it. He won't be able to dump you fast enough. He doesn't need your shit.*

"Hey. Everything okay?"

"Yeah. Of course. Everything's fine."

Pulling up to a stop light, he took a long look at her. "Why does that sound like it's not the whole story?"

"It's been a long week."

"Maybe you need a vacation."

Her short burst of laughter sounded bitter and she smiled to offset it. "Sorry. That's— You're right. Of course. I could use a vacation. Then again, I'm sure that's true of practically everyone I know. One of these days I'll take one."

Just wouldn't be any time soon.

"You sure you're okay?"

"A little tired. And maybe a little nervous about meeting your friends."

"Nothing to worry about. You're gonna fit right in."

RJ KNEW something was off with Sugar. He just couldn't get her to open up about whatever was bothering her.

The way she'd reacted when he'd said she needed a vacation kept coming back to him. Yes, there was a huge discrepancy in their financial situations. Did it matter to him? No.

Did she have a problem with it?

She'd known who he was from the moment they'd met. Hell, anyone could search his name and figure out what he was worth. She hadn't acted like it bothered her. Had he missed something?

He knew she'd been on her own for the past few years, making it work and working her ass off while she did. Nothing to be ashamed of. Hell, he admired her more than other people who had a huge bank account but had done nothing other than be born into the right family.

But he couldn't exactly come out and say that because he didn't want to embarrass her. Though she had nothing to be embarrassed about.

Shit. Why the hell was this so damn hard?

Thankfully, it didn't take long to get to Shane's place. Their conversation redirected a few times and that momentary tension dialed back. Maybe he'd imagined it. Maybe she was just nervous about meeting his friends. Which really didn't make sense because Sugar had never met a stranger.

Shane greeted them at the door, a big, quiet guy with a smile that never seemed fully formed. Unless he was smiling at his girlfriend, Bliss, whose friendly personality had already snagged Sugar and enticed her away from RJ with the promise that they'd return with drinks.

Most of the guys were already there, and he ended up talking with a few of the younger ones about their recent trip to Jamaica, keeping an eye on Sugar, who'd been absorbed into the group of women.

Most of the women had met when their guys played in Reading and were already close friends. Sugar looked as if she belonged.

"Uh, RJ? You still with us?"

"He's gone. Just ignore him. Eventually, he'll realize he's lost his ba—hey!"

Without looking, RJ reached out and smacked his brother on the back of his head, which just made Brody laugh.

"My ears still work. Watch your mouth. You know I can still take you in a fight."

"No way in hell, big brother. You're older and wiser, but I'm younger and faster."

Dragging his attention away from Sugar, he pinned his brother with a look that would've made anyone else slink off into a dark corner. Brody just smirked at him.

"And obviously not as smart. When did you get here?"

"Just a few minutes ago. Need to talk to you for a minute."

With a nod to the other guys, Brody pulled RJ to the side, his expression sobering.

"What's wrong? Did something happen?"

"Marisol's in town."

It took RJ a couple seconds to process what Brody had said and a split second to realize he didn't care.

"Last I heard, she was still in L.A. No idea why she'd be in Philly. How do you know, anyway?"

"She called me." Brody's face clearly expressed his feelings about that. And they weren't good. "Wanted me to warn you that you might cross paths. At least, that's what she said. She was absolutely fishing for information. She should've known she wouldn't get any from me. I figured it's better to let her twist in the wind, you know?"

"How many obscenities did you use when you talked to her?"

"Only a couple. You should be proud of me."

RJ was proud of Brody, just not for his restrained use of f-bombs. "Thanks for the heads-up. I can't believe she called you."

"Yeah, she must be desperate to think I'd tell her anything. She's lucky I didn't hang up on her when I realized who it was. But I figured she might call Gabby, and Gabby would rip her a new one."

RJ shook his head, covering up the fact that he wanted laugh by taking a sip of beer. His gaze never strayed from Sugar and the other women. They were laughing about something, shaking their heads and passing around a bottle of wine. Tara had her arm around Sugar's shoulders as Sugar talked to Riley Hatch's fiancée, Aly.

"She fits here." Brody nodded toward the women.

RJ glanced at Tara. "Were you worried she wouldn't?"

"I'm not talking about Tara."

Ah. "She'd fit anywhere."

"She fits *you*. When you're with her, you don't have that stick shoved so far up your ass."

RJ gave his brother another one of those looks, which, of course, Brody ignored. "We've been seeing each other for two weeks. You're getting ahead of yourself."

Brody shrugged. "You two have been in a relationship for, like, the past six months. You just made it official in the past two weeks. Just my two cents. But you know I'm right."

"When did you become—"

"Hey," Brody cut him off. "Big event's about to start."

"What?"

"Dude. You are so far out of the loop. Just shut up and watch."

Sugar returned then with a beer for him, holding a glass of wine.

Without thinking, he put his arm around her shoulders and drew her into his side, which literally made Robbie Lindback, who'd probably make the jump to the NHL from the AHL this season, gawk like he'd just seen a ghost. Which earned him an elbow in the side from his brother, Mik, who played on RJ's offensive line.

Sugar smiled up at him and RJ realized he wanted that smile for himself. He'd never felt that way about Marisol. Which was probably why they'd dated for more than two years, but he'd always shied away from taking their relationship further.

Brody was right. He'd known Sugar longer than his parents had known each other before they'd decided they were going to get married.

Sugar's smile softened and her head tilted. "What are you thinking?"

"That—"

"Hey everyone." Shane's deep voice carried through the room, immediately silencing the chatter. "Bliss and I want to thank you all for coming tonight to break in our new house. You've become part of our family and we're happy to be able to share so much of our lives with you."

"Dude, I room with you," CJ Young shouted from across the room. "We share way too much sometimes."

The guys groaned as Bliss tossed her head back, laughing loudly, and Shane just shook his head.

"Don't make me repeat the Pepto story." Shane's deadpan delivery made everyone laugh harder. "Anyway, in addition to christening the house, we've got some other news to share."

Putting one hand in his pocket, Shane withdrew a ring. From his spot across the room, RJ could tell it was an emerald solitaire. Since Bliss didn't look surprised, RJ assumed Shane had already proposed. And from the huge smile on her face, she'd apparently said yes.

When Shane slipped the ring on Bliss's finger, the room erupted in cheers and applause. Everyone converged on the couple as a group, shaking Shane's hand and hugging Bliss.

As RJ waited for his turn to talk to the couple, he glanced down at Sugar, who was holding tight to his hand. Her eyes looked wet, but her smile was bright. After they'd congratulated the couple, he pulled her to a quiet corner.

"You okay? I know these guys can be a little overwhelming—"

"I'm fine. Seriously. All girls cry at weddings and engagements. It's kind of expected."

"Is that part of the girl code?"

"Of course."

"You sure there's nothing else going on?"

She didn't say anything right away, like she was thinking over something. Finally, she shook her head. "Nothing that can't wait. Besides, we're at a party. We're not supposed to be huddled away in a corner by ourselves. Your friends just got engaged. We should be celebrating."

She wasn't wrong. But he could tell there was something on her mind.

Leaning down to speak directly into her ear, he said, "Tonight. When we're in bed, after I've made you come, I want to know what's going on."

Color flushed her cheeks, and her eyes narrowed. "Maybe I'll tell you after I've gone down on you and made you come."

His heart began to race, and his cock hardened. "You're going to pay for that."

"I can't wait."

RJ PUMPED into Sugar one last time, his cock spasming inside her as he came.

She'd already slumped down over him, her breath warm against his chest, her pussy still clenching with her own orgasm.

For several long minutes, they lay in his bed, skin fused together by the heat they'd created before he settled her next to him and got up to take care of the condom in the bathroom. When he returned, she watched him take every step. And he remembered what he'd said to her earlier.

Sliding back into bed next to her, he got them both situated under the covers.

"You ready to talk to me about what's bothering you?"

"Why do you think there's anything bothering me?"

"I may be male but I'm not blind. Something's going on. Tell me."

"I'm just thinking about making some changes in my life."

His breath caught in his chest. "What kind of changes?"

"Job changes, mostly. I have an interview with the manager at the rink tomorrow. I need to thank—"

"No. You don't. I told you about an opportunity. And I mentioned to the manager that I knew someone who might fit what she needed. I didn't do anything more than that, so don't thank me because I didn't do anything for you that I wouldn't have done for another friend."

"I still appreciate it. You don't... It just comes at a good time, especially because I want to leave Nero's."

Hell, maybe he should say something more to the manager about hiring Sugar. He'd do whatever he could to get her out of that hellhole of a club, even leverage a job for her.

And if Sugar found out he did more than tell her about a job opening? Then what? She was already skittish about it. Better to just let it ride.

"Work's been rough lately?"

"Yeah. It's always something."

"Then let me help you take your mind off your troubles."

He felt her smile against his chest as her fingers traced his jawline.

"I'm sure you can."

NINE

"Damn, Shug. You look like an honest-to-god adult. Hell, I'd hire you to run my life. Oh wait, you used to. And look what happened when left to my own devices."

In the mirror, Sugar saw Cookie pat her belly as she grinned at her sister.

"I *am* an honest-to-god adult, and I really want this job. I just don't want RJ to think I'm sleeping with him to get a good recommendation."

"Oh, please. How were you supposed to know he was going to know someone with a job that you'd be right for? Seriously, you're overthinking this whole thing."

"I don't know, Cook. What happens when we break up?"

"Are you *planning* to break up with him? I thought you liked him. Like, really liked him. I haven't met the guy, but I understand why you wouldn't want to spring your eight-months-pregnant, freeloading sister on him right away."

Sugar sliced a glare her sister's way. "You know that's not—"

"Shug. Please. Don't screw up a good thing because of me."

"I'm not screwing up a good thing. It's only been a couple of weeks." And great sex with a man who was just too good to be true. "And—"

"And you're already thinking ahead to the end. That's not like you." Cookie shook her head. "You've always been the one who made the rest of us look on the bright side. Look for the good in the situation instead of the bad. Why aren't you taking your own advice?"

Her stomach turned over, which she attributed to nervousness over her interview. "It's called being a realist. I have no idea if it's going to work." No matter how much she might want it to. "Our lives are just so different."

"Are you talking about his age? I know he's a few years old than you, but does that really matter that much? I mean, you're the oldest twenty-three-year-old I know."

"Gee, thanks. That makes me feel great."

"Okay, how about the most *mature* twenty-three-year-old I know? Does that work for you?"

"Honestly, it just makes me feel like an imposter."

"What? How so?"

"I'm just babbling. Forget that. I'm nervous. I'd really like to get this job."

"Then go kill this interview and we'll celebrate with midnight ice cream. You work 'til close tonight, right?"

"Yep." She couldn't stall anymore. She needed to leave now or she could be late. And that definitely wouldn't get her the job. "Call me if you need anything."

"Like a ride to the hospital? Who else would I call?"

Sugar turned to give Cookie a hug.

"Love you."

"Love you too." Cookie squeezed her just a little tighter. "Don't give up what you want just because you think you don't deserve it. Or him."

RJ HAD THOUGHT he might see Sugar after her interview Friday morning, but by the time noon rolled around, he figured she'd been there and gone.

Not that he would've had much time to talk to her. The kids had acted like they'd been juiced with about a metric ton of sugar and keeping them on task had been all he could manage today. Luckily, he'd had help.

"Hey, Dad, thanks again for spending the day. I really appreciate it."

"No thanks needed. I enjoyed the hell out of it. Reminds me of when you and your brother and sister were young." He rolled his shoulder as they walked together to the parking lot. "It reminds me that I was also a hell of a lot younger then too."

"You're not old."

"Didn't say I was. Then again..." He rolled his neck, laughing under his breath. "You seem to be in a better mood lately."

"Life's been good. I think...things are gonna be okay."

His dad smiled, the one only his kids saw. The one that was a little exasperated and kind of relieved and mostly just amused at the humans he'd had a hand in creating.

"Oh yeah? And how did you finally come to that conclusion?"

He didn't want to tell his dad he'd met a girl and that maybe she'd be the answer to all his problems because he couldn't lay that all on Sugar. He couldn't lay that on anyone but himself. But being with Sugar had made him realize a few things.

One, he needed to get over this funk because he was making his family worry. And two, he was sick of being alone.

"I decided I have to be."

His dad nodded. "Good. I've been worried about you. That

never really stops, no matter your kids' age. So, you gonna tell me about this girl you've been seeing?"

"Sure. What do you want to know?"

His dad's brows rose. "What? No pushback?"

"Why would I? She's a few years younger, but she's smart and sweet and we might not have a lot in common, but she fits me."

"Then when do we get to meet her?"

"Hopefully soon. She works a lot, mostly nights. She's a waitress."

"Oh."

"What?"

"No, no. Don't take me wrong. She just seems...different than your last girlfriend."

"Marisol wasn't right for me. I don't know how I didn't see that before."

"Maybe because you were looking at her through a different lens."

"What do you mean?"

"I mean maybe you were looking for someone who appeared to be a fit for what you thought you needed. Not someone who actually *is* who you need."

"You have a psychology degree to go with your Stanley Cup?"

His dad smacked him on the back of the head as RJ laughed. "I'm still your father. Don't piss me off."

"Wouldn't think of it. And I think you're actually right."

"Well, damn. Look at that. Took thirty years, but you finally realized what I've been trying to tell you all along. Now you just need to follow my advice."

"HI. Didn't think I'd see you tonight. You want some dinner?"

RJ looked up from his phone Saturday night, a smile already on his lips.

Sugar had to bite back a sigh. It just wasn't fair. She hadn't expected to see him tonight. And honestly, she was torn between giddy happiness and frustrated tension. She was happy to see him. But she needed to tell him about Cookie. She should've told him days ago, when Cookie had first shown up. And now that it'd been almost a week…

"Yeah, I can eat. I already had dinner with my dad so just an order of wings and a Coke."

"You always did like your wings."

The woman's voice came from behind Sugar, and she turned to see a beautiful brunette smiling at RJ, looking like she'd stepped off the pages of a fashion magazine. Tall and slim, she wore a fluttery, lime green wrap dress that looked like it'd been made specifically for her body and managed to reveal a decent amount of cleavage and still not look slutty. Probably cost as much as Sugar had made last week.

"Marisol. I heard you were in town. Wasn't expecting to see you."

Whoa. Sugar's attention flew back to RJ, his expression unwelcoming. Combined with the tone of his voice, RJ wasn't exactly thrilled to see this woman. Then Sugar made the connection on the name. This was RJ's ex.

"I was going to call, but I figured you wouldn't answer."

Even the woman's grimace was beautiful. She made Sugar feel like a frump, especially in the clothes she'd been wearing for the past five hours to work in a diner.

RJ glanced at Sugar then back at Marisol.

"I didn't think there was anything left to talk about." He shook his head. "We said everything we needed to say."

"At the time, yes. But…I'd like to talk now. If you don't mind."

Marisol took a few steps closer to the table, skirting around Sugar as if she was just another piece of furniture. Sugar was used to it, and worse, but right now, she wanted to lean down and kiss RJ, just to stake her claim.

Which was ridiculous. She didn't have a claim. They weren't married. They'd been having sex—great sex, yes, but still just sex—and there'd been no discussion about a future.

What future? You don't have a future. Isn't that what you've been telling yourself for days?

"I'll put that order in for you."

Sugar spun away and headed for the kitchen. She didn't want to hear any more, and she certainly didn't want to be there for the conversation Marisol apparently wanted to have.

Not stopping to check on any of her tables, she took the order into the kitchen and jammed the order slip on the carousel. Georgie glanced over her shoulder as she worked at the grill then did a double take.

"You okay, Shug? What happened?"

"Nothing. I'm fine. RJ wants an order of wings."

"Okay." Georgie drew the word out to a few syllables. "Did he tell you what kind?"

"No, but you can probably ask the woman at his booth. I'm sure she knows how he takes them."

Well, shit. Shit, shit, shit.

Every single person in the kitchen turned to look at her with the exact same expression—a whole lot of "what the fuck."

Then in unison, five heads craned to look out the window into the dining room. All except Georgie, who continued to look at her.

"Ranch," Georgie said. "It's always ranch. But you know that too."

She did. Damn it, she did. Shaking her head, she sucked in a deep breath then released it on a huge sigh.

"Sorry."

"Don't borrow trouble, Shug. It knows where to find you."

Hell, trouble had her address, her phone number, and all her passwords lately.

"I know, it's just... I guess I just wasn't expecting his ex to show up. Or to look like that. Although I guess I should've figured she would."

"Well, the way I heard the story, she dumped him. Order up."

And she still had a job to do. Picking up a tray, she loaded it down with the plates Georgie had lined up on the counter, took a deep breath, and headed back onto the floor.

RJ WATCHED Marisol slide into the booth opposite him and had to fight back the urge to get up and follow Sugar.

He had nothing to say to his ex and there was nothing she could say to him that he wanted to hear. He didn't want her half-assed apologies, if that's what she'd actually come here to do. She'd blown up their relationship more than a year ago with nothing more than a shoulder shrug and a blatantly false "it's not you, it's me" defense.

He wanted to go after Sugar, who'd disappeared back into the kitchen faster than he could tell Marisol she should leave because they had nothing to say to each other.

"I'm sure I'm the last person you want to see, but I really needed to see you, RJ. I'm in town for work and I can't stop thinking about how awful I was to you. After the years we spent together, to end it like that... I'm really ashamed of myself. I just want you to know," she reached across the table to brush his hand with her fingers, something she used to do when they were dating, "I'm sorry. I know you probably can't forgive me—"

"Water under the bridge." He cut her off before she could continue, wanting to move this conversation along so he could get her out the door without literally telling her to leave. "You didn't need to make a special trip to do this."

She blinked, a crack in her façade. She hadn't expected him to brush her off, probably because, a year ago, he wouldn't have. A year ago, he would've accepted her apology because he wouldn't have seen the calculation in her eyes. And maybe a hint of desperation.

"Actually, I'm staying not far from here and—"

"How'd you know where to find me?"

She blushed and his eyebrows arched. Marisol wasn't the kind of woman who blushed. Ever. "I might have stalked your Twitter just a little."

Her half-grin might have tugged at his heart before. It did nothing to him now. Not a damn thing. In fact, he couldn't believe it had before. He felt stupid for being taken in by her fake personality.

"Okay."

When he didn't offer up anything else, Marisol apparently decided now was the time to go big or go home.

"Anyway, I'm going to be in Philly for a few weeks. I've got a couple of modeling jobs and I thought maybe we could get together—"

"No. I'm—" He was about to say he was sorry, but he wasn't. Not for this. "I'm not available."

Another blink, as if she were processing that and it didn't quite compute.

Damn, Brody would be proud of him for the snark, even if he didn't say it out loud.

"Oh, I'm not... I didn't think... I didn't mean to make this awkward. I only wanted to say hello and to apologize."

"And you did, which I appreciate." Okay, that was a lie, but it was in service to getting her to leave as fast as she'd arrived. "But I'm sure you have other places to be."

Dark eyes wide, Marisol stared at him for several seconds before shaking her head, as if she hadn't heard him correctly. "I'm sorry, RJ. I never meant—"

"I know you didn't. I'm just not interested in hearing what you did mean."

Her lips parted as if she wanted to say something else, then they flattened. And there was the Marisol he remembered from their breakup.

"I'm sorry you feel that way." She slid out of the booth, smoothed her hands down the skirt of her dress, probably to erase any wrinkles. As if her dress would dare have wrinkles. "I've never known you to be a dick, RJ. It's not a good look on you."

She turned and headed for the door, brushing past the girl who'd just opened the door.

Shaking his head, he turned to look for Sugar. And found her just as she rushed out of the kitchen and toward the front door. Straight for the pregnant teenager who'd come in when Marisol had left.

"When did your contractions start?" Sugar asked. "Did your water break? Why didn't you call me earlier?"

"Because I wasn't sure it wasn't more of those Braxton Hicks things. Damn, it hurts, Shug."

"It'll be okay."

"I know. Just don't leave me."

"You know I won't. It's gonna be okay."

"I think we should go to the hospital. Oh god, Sugar, it really hurts."

"I know, hon. I just need to tell Georgie. Did you call Janine? She said she'd give us a ride when it was time."

Sugar turned to look back toward the kitchen, and her gaze snagged with RJ's. His thoughts had been spinning since she'd run out of the kitchen. Now his brain gained some traction and started to connect some dots.

First, the pregnant girl looked like Sugar. Sister, probably. Cousin, at the very least. Second, Sugar hadn't said a word to him. Not one word.

Why hadn't she told him?

Sliding out of the booth, he made their way over to them. With every step he took, her expression became more and more resigned.

"I'll take you."

"RJ. You don't have to—"

"My car's out front. You need a ride."

He watched her weigh her options as Georgie pushed through the doors from the kitchen.

"Janine'll be here in ten minutes. How you doing, Cookie?"

The teen grabbed Georgie's outstretched hand and squeezed. "I don't think—*uhhhh!*"

The girl groaned and bent at her nonexistent waist.

"Right." RJ walked to the front door and held it open. "I'll get my car. Meet me out front."

Sugar wanted to argue. He could see it in the way her lips flattened for a split second before she nodded.

"Thank you."

There'd be time for questions later. Right now, he needed to get a girl to the hospital before she had a baby in his car.

TEN

"Hey. Can I come in?"

Though she tried not to let it show on her face, Sugar had been dreading this visit for the past three days. Since the moment she and Cookie had walked through the doors of the maternity ward of the hospital, leaving RJ with a "Thanks for the ride" and a promise that they'd be fine by themselves.

And they had been. Baby Fox Michael had arrived five hours later, healthy and perfect and tiny and terrifying. Cookie had taken to nursing like a pro and her nineteen-year-old sister was a natural at the whole mothering thing. Which her sister had said was all thanks to Sugar.

"You were the best role model I could've had."

It'd made her cry, and then Cookie had started to cry and Fox had joined in and then they'd ended up laughing until their stomachs hurt. That had been two nights ago, a few hours after they'd walked out of the hospital with a newborn and a car seat and a ride home from Georgie and Janine. Sugar wasn't sure she or Cookie had slept more than five hours each since then.

RJ had texted a few times, but she hadn't answered. Hadn't

known what to say, even though he'd simply asked how they were.

And now...

She dredged up a smile for the man she'd missed so much, she had a constant stomachache. "Of course."

He took a step forward then stopped. "Is the baby asleep? I don't want to disturb...him?"

"He's a pretty sound sleeper so I don't think we'll wake him. And Cookie's exhausted so she could probably sleep through an earthquake right now."

RJ walked into the apartment and Sugar closed the door behind him, taking a deep breath while he couldn't see her. She'd gone over this conversation in her head so many times, she thought she'd had it completely mapped out. But now that it was here? Her brain went blank, until all she could think about were the times they'd spent in his bed. They taunted her with their specificity, and the heat that spread through her body was surely making her cheeks flush bright red.

Finally, she turned to find him leaning against the back of the couch, his expression blank. Which was way worse than if he'd been angry.

"I guess you have questions."

He nodded. "Of course. But first, is your sister okay? That was your sister, right? Kind of hard to miss the family resemblance."

"Yes. Cookie. She's the middle. And she's fine. The baby's fine. And I need to thank you for taking us—"

"I did what any decent person would do. I guess what I really want to know is why I had no idea your pregnant sister was living with you. Why didn't you tell me?"

"I don't have a good answer for that."

His arms crossed over his broad chest. "Then give me your

not-good answer. I thought we were more than just casual fuck buddies."

She flinched, the calm control in his voice worse than any curse he could've thrown at her in anger. "I didn't want to burden you with my problems."

"How would telling me your sister was pregnant and living with you burden me?"

"Because I didn't want you to think I was using you."

His lips thinned. The first crack in his composure. "Why would I even think that? What gave you the impression that I would ever think that?"

Her heart began to beat a little faster, her stomach tightening into a knot. She'd practiced this conversation in her head so many times, when she was walking the baby back to sleep at three in the morning or during her five-minute shower before she hurried off to work.

"I'm just not in a place where I can give a relationship the attention it needs. I think it's just better if we break it off now before—"

Before I start to rely on you. Care for you. Need you.

"Before what, Sugar?"

It's already too late, isn't it?

"Before we develop feelings for one another."

"It's already too late for that. I care about you. I have for months. Are you telling me you don't feel anything for me?"

"No. Of course not. You're a good friend and—"

"Friend with benefits, right?

The knife in her gut twisted a little deeper. "That's not all."

"That's kinda what it's feeling like right now."

"I like you, RJ. I just don't think I can give you what you need right now."

"And what is it you think I need?"

"More than I can give you."

There it was. As simply as she could lay it out.

His expression didn't change at all. He just continued to stare at her.

What did you expect?

Something other than this steady regard. Anger, maybe. Not…nothing.

"I don't need you to take care of me."

After a few more seconds of silence, he nodded. "Okay. And what if I want to take care of you?"

"Then I'd say that's not an equal partnership. Your ex—"

"There's a reason she's my ex, you know. Marisol would've had no problem at all asking me to take care of her and her pregnant sister and the rest of her family. Because that's the kind of person she is. That's not you, Sugar. Why is wanting to help you a bad thing?"

Her frustration was beginning to make her head spin. He had an answer for everything, and she was working on very little sleep. But she knew one thing.

"I don't want you to be with me because I need something from you."

"So you're going to work yourself into the ground because you won't accept my help."

"We have help. Georgie and Janine—"

"But you don't want *my* help."

She couldn't rely on him. She couldn't.

"You're an amazing guy. I just can't make this work right now."

She couldn't keep this up much longer because if he didn't leave now, she might cave and let him stay. And it'd be so easy for her to let him take over. And then she'd be no different than her parents.

She must have finally got through to him because after a few seconds, he stood.

"So where does that leave us, Sugar?"

Her brain just couldn't come up with the words she needed to say. Maybe because she didn't want to say them.

A little muscle at his jaw jumped.

"And if that doesn't work for me?"

She held back a wince. "You have to figure that out for yourself."

The baby cried out, a full-throated wail, her sister's soft voice softly cooing to him.

"I have to give Cookie a hand and I have to get to work."

"Sugar—"

"I'm sure we'll see each other at the diner, but I know you're going to be busy with the start of the season soon and—"

The baby wailed again, and she took a breath, ready to tell him she had to go. But the words stuck in her throat as he stepped forward, wrapped a hand around her neck, and sealed his mouth over hers.

His kiss was a brand, hot and possessive and meant to show her exactly what she'd be missing. But she really hadn't needed the reminder. She knew exactly what she was losing.

Which was why she kissed him back. She returned his passion with the fire of her own and heard him groan deep in his throat as his other arm wrapped around her waist, drawing her closer.

"Hey, Shug—oh shit." Cookie's voice barely made it through the haze of lust in Sugar's blood. "Yeah, I'll just go back in here and close the door."

RJ released her, but not without one last, hard kiss.

"I'm not ready to give this up. Are you?"

She took a step back. "I don't have a choice right now. Please don't make this situation any worse than it already is."

He looked like he wanted to say something else. Instead, he nodded and walked out the door.

It took Sugar several long seconds before she could unstick her feet from the floor.

"AND YOU HAVEN'T SEEN her since? Not even at the diner? That sucks. So what are you gonna do?"

RJ shook his head as he and Brody took a lap around the rink Thursday morning. Brody had volunteered to help run drills with the kids, who would show up in about half an hour.

Skating always helped RJ clear his head. His brother...not so much.

"I don't know what I can do."

"What the fuck does that mean?"

"It means I'm not going to force myself into a situation where I'm not wanted."

Brody slapped his stick against RJ's shin pads. "So you're just gonna give up and go home with your tail tucked between your legs? Damn, bro. You need a kick in the ass."

"She told me she doesn't want me. If I force her to accept my help, I'm doing exactly what I was accused of doing in L.A."

"Situations are totally different, and you know that."

"She flat-out told me she didn't want me there."

"Okay, so you left. But she's gotta be fucking terrified. So what are you gonna do to help?"

"I offered to help. Whatever she needs. She still told me to leave."

"Dude, you're the nicest fucking guy I know. You'd give the shirt off your back to a random guy on the street. She knows that. She doesn't want to be just another one of your charity cases. Did you tell her how you feel about her?"

"We've been seeing each other for less than a month. I'm supposed to declare my undying love?"

"Of course not. Unless, of course, you do. Then I'd get on that. But, seriously, have you *shown* her you want to help and not just told her?"

Shit. Why did that actually sound like good advice?

"Explain."

"Dude. Seriously. Send them dinner. Or breakfast. Buy the baby diapers. Don't buy shit for Sugar. Get presents for the baby and her sister. Send Sugar a gift certificate for a massage or something like that. Hell, be creative." Brody frowned at him. "Why are you looking at me like that?"

"Because those are actually good ideas."

"Fuck you. I do have a few occasionally."

RJ reached over and grabbed his brother's head and planted a kiss on his forehead, while Brody laughed.

"SUGAR DONAHUE, this is Dominque Kieriakis from the Philadelphia Iceplex. We talked last week about the assistant concession manager job. Could you give me a call when you get this?"

Friday afternoon, Sugar set her phone aside after listening to the voice message, her heart pounding, and hope a furious flutter in her belly.

"Hey, Shug, I'm gonna take Fox for a— What's wrong? What happened?"

"Nothing's wrong." Sugar turned to take the baby from her sister, snuggling the swaddled baby and rubbing her nose against his tiny little one, as she did about a hundred times a day. "I got a call back from the iceplex. They said I should call."

"What? Seriously? That's great news! When did they call?"

"Yesterday afternoon. I can't believe I missed the notification."

"You've been a little busy. I mean, what time did you get off work last night? Two a.m.? And you were up with Fox at six. Why didn't you wake me?"

"Because you need sleep, too. And I went back to bed for a few hours so I'm fine."

Cookie shook her head but didn't push it. "So call them back now. What are you waiting for? They want to hire you. They're not going to not offer you the job because you didn't call back right away."

"I know, but I've got to be downstairs in five minutes. Maybe I should wait to call Monday."

"No way. You need to call now. Give me my baby and make the call. If you get this job, that's a huge gamechanger for you. You'll have regular hours and health insurance."

"But my schedule won't be as flexible. I mean, I can still work the diner on the nights and weekends but what if you need to go to a doctor's appointment? What if we have to take Fox to the pediatrician? Maybe I shouldn't be making any changes right now. I mean—"

"Stop." Her sister's expression turned serious. "Make the call. Right this minute. You are not going to blame my baby for not taking this job."

Sugar wanted to stick her tongue out at Cookie, but she refrained. "I'm not blaming him. Maybe they just want to tell me no."

"If they didn't want you, they wouldn't have called. Call them back right now."

Sugar knew Cookie was right, even as doubts kept swirling through her mind. The only way to find out if she'd gotten the job was to call.

And if you get it?

She'd have to thank RJ. Whom she missed more than she could say. Her chest hurt, like someone had punched her in the heart. It'd been hell not seeing him. He hadn't been into the diner since he'd walked out of her apartment Tuesday.

She'd wanted to call him every day since. Had looked for him at the diner but he hadn't come in. Because of Sugar. Which sucked.

"Oh, hey, I forgot to tell you. Did you order, like, a month's supply of diapers?"

"What? No. Why?"

"Because we got ten cases of them yesterday."

"Ten cases? Was there a card or a receipt or something?"

"Nope, just ten cases of diapers sitting in the hall. Maybe Sun and Carlos?"

"They would've said something. Maybe Janine and Georgie, but why wouldn't they have told me?"

"Don't know. Don't care. They're gonna come in handy, the way this guy goes through them. I had no idea something so small could produce so much poop."

Sugar laughed as she handed Fox back to Cookie. "I'll ask around the diner."

"*After* you make the call."

After she made the call.

"YOU HUNGRY, Rickie? 'Cause I gotta warn you, I'm not much of a cook, but I do know some great places to eat."

"Oh, I don't expect you to cook for me, Mr. Mitchell. My mom taught me a few basics in the kitchen, and I picked up more from my big sister. She and her husband have their own restaurant back home. And my oldest brother, he's always running the grill when we have family parties. My dad burns pretty much anything he touches, so my mom don't let him cook much. My brothers think he does it on purpose so he never has to help, but I think he really just can't cook, and he doesn't want to admit there's something he can't do."

RJ grinned and let Rickie run at the mouth. The kid was good at that. RJ didn't know if Rickie was nervous or this was just how he was all the time. Not that it mattered. The kid was too damn nice and so stinking funny that RJ let him go.

It was nice to hear someone's voice other than his own. Since he'd walked out of Sugar's apartment last week, he hadn't been back to The Brig to eat. Hadn't wanted to run into her or cause her any added stress. Or have her ask if he was the one sending the unexpected supplies.

As far as he knew, she didn't know who was sending them, though she had to be suspicious. Whatever she thought, she hadn't called or texted to confront him so that was good.

He'd thrown himself into training, with training camp only a couple weeks away. He needed to be in shape for the start of the season in October and the preseason games would be here before he realized.

That didn't mean he didn't think about her. Every day. All the time.

The owner of the iceplex had called to thank him for pointing Sugar in her direction and told him she'd taken the job and would start next Monday. He'd wanted to call Sugar and congratulate her. He'd told her he'd give her space but, damn it, it was so goddamn hard when all he wanted to do was tell her she and her sister and the baby would be moving in with him.

"Mr. Mitchell?"

Damn, he'd totally zoned out on Rickie.

"Sorry. My mind wandered for a minute. So, you wanna get something to eat?"

"Sure."

"And Rickie, I was serious. Call me RJ. Mr. Mitchell is my dad."

The kid grinned wide as RJ pulled into a spot down the street from the diner. "Yes, sir."

RJ mock groaned. "Rickie, you're killing me. I'm not that much older than you."

"Of course. I just... I mean, it's just, I was raised to respect my—"

"Say it and you're walking back to my apartment."

RJ turned off the car and sliced a glare at Rickie, whose wide smile made RJ shake his head. It was impossible not to be ensnared in the kid's enthusiasm. From the moment RJ had picked him up at the airport, Rickie had practically vibrated out of his skin with excitement.

He got it. He did. He remembered his first rookie camp. He wasn't sure he'd slept the entire week. Even as he'd been driving to the airport, he hadn't been sure this was a good idea. He'd managed to keep his foul mood from infecting the kids at camp, but he'd basically become a hermit. He worked out, he skated, he ate dinner, he watched tv, he went to bed. And dreamed of Sugar.

"Are we eating cheesesteaks?"

"If that's what you want, that's what Georgie'll make you. Best food in the city."

"Great! I'm starving."

RJ grabbed the gift bag from the backseat, a tiny little one-piece deal with the Colonials logo on the front and the words "Newest member of the Colony." This was the first official gift he'd give the baby. The others were his probably-not-so-sneaky attempt at giving her a hand without shoving it in her face.

Gift in hand, he led Rickie to the door of The Brig. And of course, the first person he saw was Sugar.

She literally stood two feet from the door. Her eyes widened and she froze, staring up at him with her lips parted.

She looked tired. He wanted to reach across the divide and

stroke his hand down her cheek, steal a kiss, and wrap his arms around her.

Instead, he said, "Hello, Sugar. Can we get a table?"

She blinked. "Sure. Of course. Take your pick. I'll, uh, send someone over to wait on you."

He thought about sitting at one of her tables but figured she'd send another waitress anyway. So he led Rickie across the room from his normal table. It felt weird. Hell, not getting a smile from Sugar felt weird but, damn it, he needed to take this slow and not screw it up.

"I thought you were gonna take me to some fancy restaurant." Rickie grinned as they slid into opposite sides of the booth. "This is so much better."

"Not really into that kind of food. Besides, Georgie makes the best meatloaf in the world."

"Now that's the kind of compliment I like to hear. Been a while."

"Hey, Georgie." RJ nodded to the owner, who'd appeared at their table. "I've been busy." He couldn't help but slide a glance at Sugar. "I want you to meet Rickie. Rickie Prescott, Georgie Miller. This is her place."

Rickie stood and held out his hand. "Ma'am. Nice to meet you."

George took his outstretched hand, her expression serious as a heart attack. "You too, Rickie. You're the new draft pick, right?" Then she rattled off his stats, making Rickie's eyes widen. "Impressive numbers. You're gonna be a great addition to the team."

"Thank you, ma'am. Are you a fan?"

"Some of our favorite customers happen to play hockey, so yeah, we're fans. Now, you sit down, and I'll send a waitress over. Nice to meet you. And it's good to see you again, RJ."

While he tried not to follow Sugar's every move, he talked to

Rickie, learned more about the kid's family and friends, and talked about their shared love of hockey. It was close to eight at night and the crowd was light. Their food had just been delivered when Rickie popped off his seat and headed for the front door.

"Thank you so much. I'm still getting the hang of maneuvering the stroller. I swear it's worse than driving a car."

"No problem. You want me to fold that up for you? My sister has one of those."

Sugar's sister reached down and picked up the baby. "You would be my hero."

While Rickie folded up the stroller, Cookie looked around the room and stopped when she spied RJ. With a grin on her face, she made her way over to the table, after looking around the diner, probably for Sugar, who was nowhere to be seen.

RJ stood before she got there. "Cookie, right? How are you?"

"A lot better than the last time you saw me." She turned so RJ could see the baby in her arms. Yep, looked like a baby, with dark hair and perfect skin and tiny nose and lips. "This is Fox. I really want to thank you for taking us to the hospital that night. I don't know what we would've done without your help."

"Not a problem. Can you sit for a few minutes? I have something for the baby."

Cookie's grin, an exact replica of her sister's, made him long for Sugar to smile at him again.

"You didn't have to do that."

"It's just a little something."

He grabbed the bag from the bench and handed it to her. Then shook his head. "Can I hold him for you?"

Another smile, this one a little softer. "Sure. Thanks."

She put the baby in his arms and everything around him disappeared. So much responsibility in such a tiny package. It made him instantly want to shield the baby from any harm.

"I think he's pretty special, too."

RJ smiled at Cookie as she slid into the booth, the little bag in her hand, leaving RJ to sit on the end with the sleeping baby.

"He's beautiful. Congratulations."

"Thank you. And, oh my god, this is adorable!"

"Glad you like it."

"And it should fit him just in time for the season to start." Cookie looked over his shoulder before she looked back at him.

"She misses you and I'm worried she's giving up on your relationship. What are you going to do about it?"

He didn't pretend to misunderstand her. "I'm not sure yet. Got any suggestions?"

"Well, I think you're doing okay with the gifts so far. And I don't mean this." She shook the little outfit. "I don't think she figured it out until, like, a day ago. The diapers were good. Anybody could've sent those. And the grocery delivery. Don't know how you manage to get them all delivered without a receipt but, man, you're good."

He didn't nod, didn't smile, didn't acknowledge that she'd figured out that he was sending the deliveries. He considered it a win that Sugar hadn't called him out on it yet.

"So what are you going to do for an encore?"

Honestly, he didn't know. He'd been thinking it over but hadn't come up with anything that didn't end up with Sugar pushing him farther away.

As if she could read his mind, Cookie leaned forward a little.

"The baby stuff's great but don't let her forget you're hot for her."

IT WAS a good thing Sugar didn't have a tray in her hands as she stepped out of the kitchen.

Seeing RJ hold Fox might've made her drop it.

As it was, her lungs seized and her heart leaped into her throat. And every reason she'd had for telling this man she didn't need him drowned under a flood of hormones telling her to drag him back to her apartment and tie him to her bed.

Luckily, that little sarcastic voice in her head was there to set her straight.

Sure, show everyone how responsible you are. Just let him take over. Let him spend his money. Then you'll be just like his old girlfriend. That's what he wants, right?

Ugh.

"Sugar, come look what RJ brought. Isn't it adorable? Fox is gonna look so cute watching the games."

Since it was slow, and it'd be rude to outright ignore her sister, Sugar walked over to the table. Her traitorous heart flipped, but she attributed that to being tired.

As Cookie waved the cutest little pair of pajamas in Colonial colors at her, Sugar couldn't help but smile.

She had to swallow before she could say, "That's sweet of you, RJ. Thank you."

"Gotta grow fans young, right, Rickie?"

"Uh, yeah?"

The young guy with RJ was obviously another hockey player. Big and muscled but still young enough to be considered a kid.

"Rickie, this is my sister, Sugar." Cookie covered a yawn. "Ugh. Sorry. Existing on a few hours of sleep every night is starting to catch up with me. So I'm gonna take the little guy here and head up to bed. Thanks again for the gift, RJ. It's very cool."

RJ slid out of the booth and handed over the baby when

Cookie stood and reached for him. Then her sister gave her the look. "Don't let me sleep tonight, Sugar. You need to get some rest, too."

Then Cookie left, and Sugar and RJ stood looking at each other, only a couple of inches separating them. She was exhausted, and she knew it showed on her face in the dark circles under her eyes that not even makeup could hide completely.

He probably figured he was glad to have dodged a bullet when she told him she couldn't see him anymore. And since he hadn't even attempted to contact her in the past week, she assumed it really was over between them. And now here he stood, staring at her like they'd never shared a bed and he'd made her cry out his name as she came.

"You okay, Sugar?"

Shaking her head, mainly to stop her brain from telling her how stupid she was to still be lusting over him, she took a step back. "Sure. I'm fine. Thank you for the gift."

He nodded, his gaze taking her in from head to toe and back again. "Not a problem. How are you and Cookie getting along with the baby?"

"It's been great. An adjustment, but he's amazing." Absolutely true. "We're both just a little tired. I've got to get back to work. Your food'll be up soon. Have a good night."

She certainly wouldn't. Which proved to be true an hour later, when she dropped a full tray of dirty dishes. Luckily, RJ and Rickie had left by then and there was only one customer in the diner, and he was in the midst of paying.

Georgie walked out of the kitchen, just as she picked up the tray.

"I'm really sorry. I don't know what happened. I'll pay—"

"Stop right there." Georgie took the tray out of her hands

and set it on the counter then led her to a seat at the counter. "We need to talk."

Sugar's eyes widened at the tone in Georgie's voice.

"Now, don't look at me like that. I'm not firing you. But you need to make some changes or you're going to burn out and not be any help to anyone. Sometimes, you need to ask for help."

"I so appreciate everything you've done for us—"

"I'm not talking about me and Janine. Have you called your parents yet?"

Sugar's immediate grimace was all the answer Georgie needed.

"That's what I thought. Look, I consider you more than an employee, you know that, right? And I truly believe everyone is entitled to their privacy. But some things you just can't do on your own. Besides, I think if I had children and they didn't tell me I was a grandparent, I'd feel like I'd been shot through the gut. Everyone needs help sometimes. You're lucky you've got people willing to give you a hand."

Georgie's words followed Sugar all the way back to her apartment. Opening the door as quietly as she could, she found Cookie asleep on the couch with Fox in his carrier on the floor in front of her. The TV was on, but the sound was muted. They'd found he slept better in the carrier. Sometimes. They were still figuring out this whole baby thing. And, so far, they seemed to be doing okay.

But Georgie's comment about their parents had struck deep.

"Sugar?" Cookie pitched her voice low so she didn't wake the baby. "Everything okay?"

Sugar shook her head. She couldn't catch her breath and she couldn't find the words she needed to use.

"I think I fucked up."

Yawning, Cookie sat up on the couch, shaking her hair out

of her face. "About RJ? Yeah. Gotta agree on that one. You need to—"

"Not just RJ. But yeah. Him too. We need to call Mom and Dad."

Cookie's brows arched. "Do we have to?"

"Yes. They're going to be hurt, and that's my fault. We should've—"

"No. This isn't all on you." Cookie's tone held a hard note. "If I'd wanted to call, I would have. I just...don't know what to say. Did something happen after I left? Is everything okay? Did RJ tell you?"

"Tell me what?"

Cookie's nose wrinkled, a sure sign she was about to lie. "Nothing. Not important right now. I know we should call Mom and Dad. I've known since the minute we left the hospital. I just don't know what to say."

Sugar sat next to her sister on the couch and grabbed her hand. "We'll do it together. We'll figure it out."

"I know. But what about RJ? I don't think you want me to be on that call."

"I'm not sure it would matter. He didn't seem too thrilled to see me earlier."

"Well, you did kinda dump him for your pregnant sister. But, seriously, you honestly don't know where the diapers and the groceries and that case of baby wipes came from?"

Sugar had had her suspicions, but there'd been so much more to think about. Working eight to ten hours every day while helping Cookie with the baby had been more of a strain than she'd expected. Honestly, she hadn't known what to expect, and that had frustrated her to the point of tears. But she couldn't tell Cookie that because her sister had just had the baby and needed her to be strong.

"Did he tell you he sent them?"

Cookie rolled her tired eyes. "Of course not. You basically told him you didn't want anything to do with him and that he should butt out."

"I don't know how to fix that."

"You will. I have faith. Now go get some sleep while you can because this little guy is going to be screaming his head off in about two hours. Tomorrow, we'll suck it up and call Mom and Dad. Love you, Shug."

"Love you too."

"COOKIE, they're here. And they brought everyone. And I mean everyone."

Looking out the window onto the street in front of their house late Friday morning, Sugar watched as her parents' SUV disgorged people like a clown car. Their parents, three sisters, and, amazingly, two aunts, one from each side of the family.

Cookie stepped up to the window and huffed. "Damn, forgot Aunt Rose and Aunt Josephine were staying with them this summer. This should be fun."

The bell rang, and she and Cookie both sighed at the exact same time. Then they laughed as Sugar pressed the button to let the horde in.

She wondered if Sun and Carlos thought the building was being invaded, they were so loud. If only they'd be so lucky. This might be worse.

A deep breath and Sugar opened the door just as her youngest sister, Taffy, hit the top step.

"Sugar!"

Her voice reverberated off the walls of the short hall, but all Sugar saw was the sheer joy on her youngest sister's face as she ran toward her. Fifteen, tiny, and covered in freckles from head to toe, Taffy threw herself at Sugar and hugged her so tight, Sugar thought she'd crack a few ribs, but she didn't tell her sister to stop.

"I missed you! I feel like I haven't seen you in forever. I'm so glad to see you—Cookie!"

And for the next ten minutes, Sugar felt like she was inside that clown car as she hustled everyone inside the apartment, praying their neighbors forgave them for the chaos that ensued. Nine people talking over each other and at each other. Her mom, who'd commandeered the baby the second she walked through the door, cooing at Fox, her dad talking to her aunts, who were alternately cross-examining Cookie and trying to get their hands on the baby, and her sisters holding multiple conversations with everyone.

It was almost enough to make Sugar homesick.

Almost.

For fifteen minutes, she watched from the perimeter, not really participating because no one was there to see her. But then her mom handed the baby over to the aunts and began looking around the room until she found Sugar.

She'd never seen that look on her mom's face before, and she had no idea what it meant. What she did understand was the head nod toward the door. Mom wanted to talk.

Sugar and her mom slipped out the door without anyone noticing. Standing in the hall, Sugar expected her mom to be pissed. Hurt. Upset.

"How are you, Sugar baby?"

The pet name her parents had used as a child knocked a chink out of the wall she'd built around her heart since the moment she and Cookie had called home. As did the smile on her mom's face. It was...apologetic.

"I'm fine. I am sorry we didn't call soon—"

"Your dad and I didn't make it easy for you, did we?"

The question was so far out of left field that Sugar frowned as her brain tried to formulate a response. Before she could, her mom continued.

"We're really very proud of you, you know. I don't think we've ever told you that. You're strong and smart. You're also stubborn and headstrong, but I guess that's what kept you going all this time."

"Mom, what—"

"You never asked for much. But we should've known better and I'm sorry. You were always a better parent to your sisters than we were, and we took advantage of that."

Since it was true, Sugar shrugged, uncomfortable with the direction her mom was taking the conversation. She didn't want or need a true confessions moment. Didn't want to have to tell her mom she forgave her faults and absolved her of all wrongdoing. She'd grown up, moved out, moved on. It didn't mean anything now.

"But, sweetheart, you get to have a life, too."

"I have a life. Here. And Cookie and I will be fine—"

"We're going to take her home with us, if she wants to come."

Sugar blinked, feeling like her mom had ripped the floor out from under her feet.

"You're twenty-three, Sugar baby. You have your own life to live. We'll help Cookie get on her feet and figure out what comes next."

"But...we don't need help."

"Everybody needs help. I had you." Her mom's smile was an exact replica of Cookie's. And Sugar's. "It's time for us to return the favor. Though it's not really a favor. This is what parents are supposed to do. Take care of their children."

"We're doing fine on our own."

"Cookie mentioned that you've been seeing someone. Don't you want more time to—"

"We're not dating anymore." Sugar's head started to spin at the left turn the conversation had taken. "It's not—"

"Does the fact that you're working three jobs and taking care of your sister and her newborn have anything to do with that?"

"No. It just wasn't going to work out."

Her mom didn't respond right away, but Sugar could tell she was formulating a reply. Probably something Sugar didn't want to hear.

"Why don't we—"

"Honey, you can't keep everyone at arms' distance. Everybody needs somebody."

"That's not what happened."

"So you didn't get along?"

She shrugged, wanting this conversation to be over. Right now.

"Or you did get along, but it got too hard?"

"You don't know anything about it."

"But I know you, Sugar, better than you think I do. Not every man is going to break your heart like Bobby did. And taking on more responsibility isn't a substitute for a relationship."

Every word her mom said knocked another stone out of that wall, each stone landing like a blow.

Her mom laughed ruefully, shaking her head. "You forget I have a master's degree in psychology." Her mom wrapped her in a hug, which melted a little more of that wall. "You're only twenty-three. You deserve to have a life. Just something to think about. Now, we should go back in before your dad realizes we're gone and wants to add his two cents. The man is much better with engines than he is with people."

"WASN'T SURE YOU'D COME." Brody raised an eyebrow at him as he watched RJ slide into their usual booth at The Brig. "Thought about suggesting we meet somewhere else, but I figured you're an adult. You can handle it."

Yep, that was him. "It's fine. We're good. I saw her a couple days ago. No fireworks. Besides, she started that new job at the ice complex today. Doubt she's working here tonight."

At least, he hoped she wasn't. He didn't want her to think he was stalking her. Even though he might be.

"You would be right. She's not here. So how've you been?"

Honestly, he sucked. He missed Sugar. Missed talking to her, missed seeing her. Missed kissing her and having her in his bed.

"I'm good."

"No, you're not. You look like shit and you're grumpy."

"Says the King of Bad Moods. I'm fine, Brody. Let it go."

Picking up the menu he didn't need, RJ let his gaze drift over it, because if he didn't, he'd bite Brody's head off. And that wouldn't be fair. This was just Brody being Brody. He should be used to it after twenty-eight years.

"Yeah, right. If it was me running around looking like I'd run over my best friend and killed him a few times, you'd be all over my ass. So you can thank me later."

RJ didn't even bother to look up. "Thank you for what?"

"For lying to get you here. Don't take it all out on me, though. Tara was in on it too."

Brody slid out of the booth, making RJ scowl up at him. But the scowl dismantled in seconds when he saw Sugar walking through the door. She spotted him immediately, her lips parted in surprise. Then she blinked and flashed a look at Brody that promised retribution.

Still, she didn't look pissed. So that was a good start.

Whatever Brody had done to get her here, RJ would definitely thank him later.

His heart started to pound as she crossed the room, giving Brody an elbow in the side as he passed her. Brody just laughed and walked out the door. At eight o'clock on a Monday night, the diner set to close in an hour, there were only two other couples in the place.

He wouldn't have cared if it'd been standing room and everyone was staring at them. He only had eyes for Sugar.

"Hey."

"Hi."

He was so damn happy to see her, he just stood there, staring down at her for several seconds before he realized how ridiculous they probably looked.

"You wanna sit?"

Surprisingly, she smiled, a slow, kind of shy curve of her lips. And that tiny kernel of hope in his heart began to explode.

"Sure. If you don't mind."

"Apparently I'm not meeting my brother for food, so no, I don't mind."

"Isn't Rickie with you?"

"No. He's going out with a few of the other guys for dinner and to hang out and do whatever eighteen-year-olds do nowadays. He'll be back at my place by eleven."

As she slid into the booth opposite him, he let his gaze rake over her. She wore blue pants and a plain white shirt, a little makeup that made her eyes bigger and greener than they already were, a thin gold chain around her neck and gold hoops in her ears. He didn't know that he'd ever seen her wear jewelry before, which was a strange observation to make now.

"You started at the ice complex today, right?"

Nodding, she began to twist her hands together on the

tabletop before making a conscious effort to stop. "Yeah. I want to thank—"

"No. You don't have to. I told you before, I wouldn't have recommended you if I didn't think you were right for the job."

Her lips curved in a quick smile before it disappeared. "I know that now. I'm sorry I didn't believe in you before. I just... had some issues to work through."

The tone of her voice made his lungs tighten a little more with anticipation. Even though he knew he shouldn't get his hopes up.

"How are Cookie and the baby?"

"Good. They left Saturday to go home with my parents." His arched eyebrows made her nose wrinkle. "It's the best thing for Cookie and the baby right now. And for me. Especially starting this new job and taking a couple of credits toward my degree this fall."

"Sounds like you're going to be busy."

He needed to bring his expectations back under control. Even if he'd already started planning how he was going to win her back eventually. He may be fast on ice, but if she needed him to take it slow, he'd put on the brakes.

"I am. But this is a good kind of busy."

She looked happy, happier than the last time he'd seen her. Which was great. That's what he wanted for her, right?

Then take a step back and let her be happy.

"Good." What the hell else should he say? She looked like she was waiting for something, though. Or maybe she was just looking for an opening to leave.

"You start training camp next week, right?"

She wanted to do small talk? Okay, as long as she sat across from him and let him stare at her, he could do small talk.

"Yeah."

"Are you looking forward to it?"

"Yeah." *Do you want her to leave? Jesus, you're not normally this much of an asshole.* "I'm always excited for a new season to start. I'm ready to get on the ice and play."

"I guess you'll be pretty busy."

"Yeah." *Fuck it.* "Would you like to come to the first game? I'll get you tickets. You can sit in the arena or in the family box."

When she didn't decline right away, he studied her closer. Her cheeks were flushed, her eyes a little wide, and she was constantly worrying her bottom lip with her teeth. Nervous? Or anxious to get away? Damn it, he was gonna smack Brody for putting her in this position.

He shook his head, gaze slicing away. "Hey, sorry, I don't—"

"Yes. I would love to come to the game."

His gaze arrowed back to hers. The blush on her cheeks had gotten a little deeper, but the look in her eyes was...encouraging. Hopeful.

"Great. That's great."

"Great."

Hell. Just ask. "Would you like to go to dinner after the game?"

Her lips curved in a quick smile. "Sure."

Don't push.

"Would you like to go to dinner tomorrow?"

Her gaze dropped for a second. "I can't tomorrow. I'm still picking up a few shifts here and at Breyers, just until I'm sure this job is working out. I need to do this on my own."

No, she didn't. He wanted to tell her that, to make her understand that he wouldn't let her hand out to dry on her own. That he'd be here for her. But he also knew he couldn't push her. IF he pushed, she'd run. She'd done it already.

"I'm sure you're going to be great at it. But I understand."

Guess he'd be eating here for the foreseeable future.

He'd give her as much time and space as she needed, even if it took all freaking season.

———

"SUGAR, when are you going to put that poor guy out of his misery? He's been here every night, just waiting to get a glimpse of you."

Sugar tied her apron around her waist Monday night as she raised an eyebrow at Anika.

"He comes here to eat after training camp. Not to talk to me."

Anika gave her a look. "Uh huh. You just keep thinking that."

Sugar was beginning to think maybe RJ was getting over her. She'd been running herself into the ground all last week, working all day learning the ropes at the ice complex then putting in a few hours every night either here at The Brig or at Breyers. She hadn't wanted to leave anyone short-handed. Her boss at Breyers had hired a new waitress, so Sugar's final night there had been last week.

She'd thought about calling RJ Saturday, asking if he wanted to get together, but she'd been behind on schoolwork and had needed to catch up on that during the hours she wasn't working here.

And of course, the Colonials training camp had started last week, so RJ had been just as busy.

But Anika was right. He'd been here every night. And he always had a smile for her. Never overtly sexy but still hot enough to make her thighs clench.

She missed him. Missed knowing she could kiss him or touch him whenever she wanted. She didn't have that right anymore. But every night alone in bed, she realized she wanted to be able to touch his hand or pull him down to kiss him.

As if he was truly hers.

And yet...

Looking out the passthrough to the dining room, she could just barely see his shoulder.

"Shug, just go talk to him." Anika swatted her on the ass with a dishrag, making Sugar chuckle. "Or I'll be aiming the next rag at your head."

Laughing now, Sugar shook her head as she made her way toward his table. It wouldn't hurt to talk to him. Just for a little. Besides, it was a slow night.

"Hi—Oh my god, what happened to your *eye?*"

It was a good thing she didn't have a tray in her hands, she would've dropped it. Reaching for his chin, she gripped it with one hand as she turned his head to the side. The skin around his left eye was yellow and swollen. It'd surely be a horrible shade of black and blue by tomorrow.

"Can you see? Did you see a doctor?"

"Sugar, I'm—"

"You can't play like that, can you?"

"It's fine—"

"You don't have any broken bones, do you?"

She could barely breathe, and she knew she was making a scene, but she couldn't help it. He was hurt.

"Sugar. I'm fine. Seriously." He covered her hand on his chin with his and drew it away but didn't release her. "I've had worse. Nothing's broken. I took a puck to the face. It happens. Yeah, it looks bad, and it's gonna hurt for a while, but I'll survive."

"Do you need some ice? What can I do? God, I'm so sorry, I didn't mean to embarrass you—"

"You're not embarrassing me. Sit down, hon. You look like you're gonna pass out."

She felt helpless and stupid for making a scene. But he was right, she felt a little light-headed. Which was totally ridiculous. He was the one who'd been hurt.

"Sugar. Indulge me. Sit down."

She did as he asked, sliding into the booth opposite him, still feeling stupid.

"I'm sorry. I don't know why I went off like that."

Yes, you do. You know exactly why. And I think it's okay that you finally tell him.

Could she? Did she have the guts?

"Don't apologize." RJ grinned at her, making her stomach do little flip flops. "I think you just made my day."

SUGAR'S GAZE shot back to RJ's, her eyes wide and her expression clearly dumbfounded. He could just see the questions rolling through her brain.

"What? How?"

RJ figured she probably wanted to add, "Are you insane?" to her line of questioning but was biting her lip to keep it from spewing out.

For the past couple of weeks, he'd been wondering if she'd been having second thoughts about him. Every night he'd been here, she'd seemed farther away emotionally. He hadn't been quite sure how to handle it.

Reaching across the table, he took her hands in both of his, laced their fingers together and leaned forward so they were eye to eye. And what he saw made his heart pound furiously.

"Because you just freaked out about my black eye. Just so

you know, this is kind of a common occurrence for hockey play-ers. Going forward, you're gonna have to get used to it."

"I don't…What?"

"Since I plan to be spending a lot of time with you in the future, you should probably get used to the fact that I'm going to get hurt. Bruises. Sprains. Strains. Fractured bones. Broken bones. Torn ligaments. There're going to be days I look like I survived a gang beating."

Her eyes continued to widen until he was sure they couldn't get any bigger. He reached across the table and ran a finger down her cheek and watched her eyes flutter and her lips part.

He had to tamp down the urge to drag her across the table and onto his lap so he could kiss her. Like, really kiss her. Tongues dancing, teeth clashing, can't breathe kissing. The kind that would get them kicked out of this place.

Which wouldn't be a bad thing right now.

"So, you're going to have to get used to that. Because, Sugar…"

She sucked in a breath. "Yeah?"

"I want you there with me. Through it all."

She blinked.

"I want to come home to you at night and wake up with you in the morning. I want to be there when you graduate from college and I want you to be cheering at my games. I want—"

"I want that, too. I'm sorry—"

"No. No apologies. No 'I'm sorry.' Do you want me, Sugar?"

She nodded, her lips curving in a smile. "More than anything. Black eyes and all. But I am sorry for pushing you away. I pushed you away. I wasn't honest with you or myself about how I felt, and I made you think I didn't want you. And that's totally not true. I do want you. And I really hope—"

He slid out of the booth so he could lean down and kiss her.

It definitely wasn't an appropriate kiss for a diner, even one with only a few customers. Too much tongue and heat. Then again, when Sugar wrapped her arms around his neck and stood so she could press herself against him, someone started clapping and Georgie yelled something from the kitchen that he couldn't quite make out but sounded like, "Jesus, about damn time."

He kissed her until neither of them could breathe and he had to stop so they could.

"Come home with me, Sugar. If you haven't figured it out yet, I love you. I have never said that to another woman." He threaded his fingers through her hair and tugged her head back so he could look into her eyes, pleased to see they were glassy with desire. "And I can wait--"

"I love you, too."

"Then come home with me, Sugar."

Her smile lit up his life.

"My place is closer."

Her smile threatened to make him grab her and run out the door. He wouldn't care who was watching.

He leaned down to speak right into her ear. "I'll give you a head start."

"I'm not running anymore."

"But I'm still going to chase you, Sugar. Always."

THERE'S MORE sexy hockey players in the Redtails Hockey Romance series. Don't miss them! Start with The Brick Wall because it's free!

ABOUT THE AUTHOR

Stephanie Julian is a USA Today and New York Times bestselling author of contemporary and paranormal romance.

Stay in touch for all new releases and sales by signing up at www.stephaniejulian.com

Reserve My Nights

Expose My Desire

Keep My Secrets

Rock My Heart

LOVERS UNDERCOVER

Lovers & Lies

Sinners & Secrets

Beauty & Brains

Thieves & Thrills

FORGOTTEN GODDESSES

What A Goddess Wants

How to Worship A Goddess

Goddess in the Middle

Where A Goddess Belongs

DARKLY ENCHANTED

Spell Bound

Moon Bound